BEA
c.1

Beatty, Patricia.

The Staffordshire
Terror

DATE			

THE STAFFORDSHIRE TERROR

BY PATRICIA BEATTY

Published by William Morrow and Company
The Bad Bell of San Salvador
Billy Bedamned, Long Gone By
Blue Stars Watching
Bonanza Girl
By Crumbs, It's Mine!
Hail Columbia
How Many Miles to Sundown
I Want My Sunday, Stranger!
Just Some Weeds from the Wilderness
Lacy Makes a Match
A Long Way to Whiskey Creek
Me, California Perkins
The Nickel-Plated Beauty
O the Red Rose Tree
The Queen's Own Grove
Red Rock over the River
Rufus, Red Rufus
The Sea Pair
Something to Shout About
Squaw Dog
Wait for Me, Watch for Me, Eula Bee

Published by The Caxton Printers, Ltd.
Indian Canoe-maker

Published by McGraw-Hill Company
The Lady from Black Hawk

Patricia Beatty

THE
STAFFORDSHIRE
TERROR

William Morrow and Company / New York / 1979

Copyright © 1979 by Patricia Beatty

All rights reserved. No part of this book may be reproduced or utilized in any form or by any means, electronic or mechanical, including photocopying, recording or by any information storage and retrieval system, without permission in writing from the Publisher. Inquiries should be addressed to William Morrow and Company, Inc., 105 Madison Ave., New York, N. Y. 10016.

Library of Congress Cataloging in Publication Data

Beatty, Patricia
  The Staffordshire Terror

  Summary: The Staffordshire terrier 13-year-old Cissie raises from an orphaned pup is stolen by her uncle and entered in illegal dogfights.
  [1. Dogfighting—Fiction. 2. Family problems—Fiction] I. Title
PZ7.B380544St [Fic] 79-21787
ISBN 0-688-22201-3
ISBN 0-688-32201-8 lib. bdg.

Printed in the United States of America.
1 2 3 4 5 6 7 8 9 10

Contents

1
Small Spook

"Look out for the dog! *Look out!*" Cissie cried, as she grabbed her father's arm.

Walt Rose shrugged off her hands and spun the wheel of their pickup truck to the right on the country highway.

"I see it. Look at that crazy animal!" he shouted to his daughter.

Cissie covered her face with her hands, then cringed as a soft thudding sound followed the instant after.

Walt Rose slammed on the brakes, cut the engine, and turned angrily to the thin, sandy-haired, thirteen-year-old girl sitting next to him. "Don't you know better than to grab at a person like that when he's driving a car? I saw that blasted animal, too. It just stood there like it was crazy, like it was waiting for something. It didn't even try to get out'a my way. Craziest coyote I ever heard of. I had to hit the thing!"

"I don't think it was a coyote, Dad."

Cissie dropped her hands. "It was a dog, a gray, coyote-colored dog. It wasn't shaped like a coyote."

Her father grunted. "I say it was a coyote. Well, whatever it was, it could have wrecked us. We're on the shoulder of the road right now. Just look out your window, and you'll see we ain't more than a foot from the edge of a gully. Now let's get on home and not worry about that old coyote."

"I still think it was a dog." Cissie looked at her father out of troubled hazel eyes.

He sighed. "You want me to go take a look, huh? Is that it? You want me to see how bad it's hurt?"

"Please, Dad."

"All right, if it'll ease your mind. I was going pretty fast when we hit it, so I'm sure it's dead. If it is, I'll haul it over to the side of the road out of the way of other cars. You stay in here." Rose reached up onto the shelf behind the seat for the work gloves he kept there and put them on. Then he opened the door and stepped out.

Cissie hunched her shoulders and took in a deep breath. "Don't let it be a dog out there," she whispered. "Don't let it be a dog!"

In only a minute or so her father came back. To her surprise he didn't get into the car. He came around and opened her door, saying, "We've got something to do out there."

"Was it a coyote, Dad?" Cissie asked hopefully.

Her father shook his head. "No, cuss the luck. You were right. It was a dog. Get out, I'll get the rifle from the shelf. Don't look at me like that. The dog's dead."

"Then what do we want a rifle for?" Cissie stayed in the car.

"Rattlesnakes, mostly. Don't worry. I don't have to shoot the animal to put it out of its misery. We have to do some scouting around, though. What direction would you say the dog was coming from?"

"Over there, Dad." Cissie pointed to the right.

"Okay, that's where we'll look then."

"Look for what?" Cissie got out to stand on the edge of the road. Though it was warm that day and she was dressed in tennis shoes, jeans, and her brother's plaid shirt, she shivered.

"For any pups the dog might have had. It was a female, and I could see she was nursing pups. I put her down into the bushes on the other side of the road."

"What kind of dog was she, Dad?"

Rose shook his head. "I don't know. I never saw one like her in build and shape of the head."

"Maybe she was one of the wild dogs that run in packs down in the river bottom?"

Walt Rose looked at his daughter and shook his

11

head. "I don't think so. She was wearing this fancy collar." He pulled a dog collar out of his jacket pocket and held it out. "Go on, take it. There ain't any blood on it."

In spite of what he said, Cissie took the collar gingerly. She turned it in her hands, looking at the four tags dangling from it. It was deep red leather, and there was a silver plate set in the leather. The tags were dog licenses, not name identifications, but there was something engraved on the plate in the collar. She rubbed dust off to make out the words, *Fame's Folly.* It sure was a queer name for a dog to have. She said, "I wonder how a dog who belongs to somebody ever got way out here. It's miles from town, Dad."

"Yep, and not many folks travel on this old road anymore because of the new freeway. This road only goes to our place and the reservoir, and then it dead-ends in the hills."

He stood ready with the rifle tucked under his arm. "Come on. Let's look for puppies. If there are any out there, I don't want coyotes or buzzards gettin' them. It was bad enough hitting the female. Remember, don't run on ahead in case I trip and the rifle fires by accident. Watch out for snakes on top of the rocks. It's getting close to sundown, and that's the time of day they like."

"Sure, Dad. Do you think there *are* pups out there?" Cissie waved her arm toward the rolling countryside, strewn with small green bushes and boulders.

"Maybe so, unless whoever lost the female or dumped her out of a car kept the pups."

"Dumped her?" Cissie stared at her father.

"Maybe so. Folks do dumb things sometimes, you know. They figure a dog they don't want or can't afford to feed can make its way alone in the country-side. Let it go wild. But that ain't easy for a pet animal, not even here in California where the weather's warm most of the time. It would be worse in Arkansas."

"I hope there are puppies, and I hope we can find 'em, Dad."

The short, balding man and the girl went down into the gully at the road's edge and from there up onto the plain under sharp-peaked, rocky hills. They walked in silence, the man now and then pausing to stop and listen.

After a time he pointed to the west. Cissie split off from him, walking carefully and slowly, staring at the ground, then stopping and listening, too. She saw nothing but a swift-moving yellowish lizard scurrying away in front of her and darting under the overhang of a little boulder. Although Cissie hadn't spotted any puppies yet, her father was gen-erally right about things that had to do with ani-mals. The only reason he had mistaken a dog for a coyote was that his eyes weren't as good as hers.

His yelling at her about grabbing his arm was just a cover-up for how bad he felt about hitting the dog. No matter how he'd talked, he wouldn't have liked hitting a coyote either. Cissie let out a deep sigh, thinking about the dead dog up on the road.

Today hadn't been a good day at all. First she had spent the whole Saturday afternoon with the dentist having four teeth filled, and now Dad had hit a dog. She sighed once more.

Her sigh was answered by a small sound, a high whimpering. It was so soft a sound that it couldn't be far away. Where had it come from? From a puppy? Cissie whistled very softly, then called out, "Doggie, doggie." She stood stock-still to listen.

When the whimper came again after a moment of waiting, Cissie started toward a tumbleweed bush on her right. She walked carefully, setting her feet just so and moving as quietly as she could.

There it was, huddled into a whitish ball under the tumbleweed. Kneeling down, Cissie picked up the tiny puppy, holding it in both of her hands while it squirmed and wriggled. Swiftly she looked around for other pups. No, just one puppy. That was all there was. One puppy and what was left of a rabbit, the food the female must have killed and brought here to eat.

Cissie said to the fuzzy pup. "Your mama was out hunting again, but she won't be back this time.

You're gonna go home with me. You sure can't stay out here!"

She got to her feet, still holding the puppy in both hands. "Dad," she cried, "Dad, I found it! I found the puppy. I got him. He's all right."

Walt Rose didn't shout in return. He waved his arm toward the pickup and started back toward it. Cissie followed him. Wary of falling on the rocky, uneven ground and injuring the tiny pup, she threaded her way with care among the bushes and rocks.

When she got to the truck where her father waited, she lifted her hands to display the dog and said, "He doesn't act one bit scared of me, Dad. He didn't wiggle much, and now he's cuddled down just fine."

Mr. Rose looked at the puppy and said, "He ain't old enough to be scared of anything yet, Cissie. That takes time for man or beast to learn. He's colored like his mother, a sort of whitish-gray." He laughed. "A sort of spooky coyote color."

Cissie smiled. "That's what I'll call him. Spook! What kind of dog is he?"

"I dunno. It's hard to tell about a pup. Maybe he's the same kind his mother was, but I don't know what she was either. Come on, get in."

"Oh, Dad, do you think we can keep him?"

"Maybe. We've got just about everything else

15

that has four legs on our place. Let's get on home with the grub your mother asked for. She'll be wanting some of it for supper."

Cissie didn't hear his talk about groceries. Absorbed in the ball of fur in her hands, she was thinking that this was the very first dog they'd ever had that would be her own.

All at once Walt Rose said, "Cissie, let's tell your mama that somebody gave you the puppy at the dentist's office. It'd grieve her if she heard about our pickup hitting the dog's mother by accident. There's no cause to trouble your mother; she's had enough trouble already. It'd upset Lita, too."

"Sure, Dad. I won't tell 'em. But what about the collar in your pocket?"

"I'll hide that away in the barn. We'll look in the newspaper to see if anybody advertises for a lost gray female with a pup. We ought to do that, you know."

"Dad, would we have to give the puppy back to them?"

"Yes, and then we'd have to tell your mama the true story no matter what. We couldn't keep somebody else's pup. I don't want any trouble hereabouts, Cissie. Things are going just fine for us now. We've been here quite a time, and I still like taking care of Mr. Benson's property while he lives in town. I don't want anybody saying that we stole a dog or anything else. We don't want any trouble with the law."

~ Cissie nodded. "Do you think there'll be anything in the papers about the female?"

"I dunno. You keep watch so we don't miss it if there is."

Again Cissie nodded. "Okay, Dad. Darrell, Lita, and I like it here, too."

Walt Rose grinned at his girl. "We're doing just fine here in Mira Loma, better than we ever done. We don't owe any bills, we pay cash, and we mind our own business."

Holding the puppy to her chest, Cissie slid along the seat to nestle her head on her father's shoulder as he drove. "Some folks we used to know other places won't find us out here either, will they, Dad?"

"I sure hope not, honey."

Though the Benson place was a treasured home to Walt Rose and his family, it wasn't much to look at. It consisted of an old two-story wooden house, a barn across from it, a cluster of sheds, and among them a windmill. The house needed paint and the railings on the porch needed some shoring up, but there was a trellis covered with fragrant yellow honeysuckle, and scarlet geraniums bordered the front of the porch.

Everybody was there to greet the battered blue

pickup as it bounced over the ruts in the old private Benson road to a stop in front of the house.

Shirley Rose called out to her husband, "Walt, did you remember to get the cornmeal?"

"I got it," he shouted back, "and everything else you put on the list." He waved to the thin, sharp-featured woman in blue jeans and striped blouse, whom Cissie closely resembled.

Lita Helms, Cissie's cousin, got up out of the porch swing where she'd been sitting with ten-year-old Darrell Rose. At the top of the steps she leaned against a post, posing.

Cissie grinned. Lita, age seventeen, was funny. This year she was a blonde and thin. Last year she'd been a redhead and plumpish. She changed herself a lot.

Lita called out, "How did it go with Dr. Fang, Cissie?"

Cissie got out of the truck with the puppy cradled to her chest. "It was okay," she said. "It didn't hurt. He gave me novocain or something. See what I brought home with me!" She held the tiny dog up to be seen.

Sturdy, freckled Darrell shouted, "What you got there, Cissie?"

"A puppy." Coming up on the porch, Cissie told her white lie. "One of the ladies in the dentist's office gave it to me. I told her last time I was there that we had cats and dogs and a horse and sheep and a goat and chickens and used to have ducks, too. Dad says I can keep Spook."

"Spook? What kind of name is that?" Darrell came over to stare at the puppy.

Cissie explained. "He's sort of a ghostly, spooky color, isn't he?"

By now all of the Roses and Lita had gathered around Cissie, looking at the puppy.

Mrs. Rose asked, "What kind of dog is it?"

"I dunno, Mom. I forgot to ask the lady."

Lita sniffed. "If somebody just gave it away, it's probably eighty-seven kinds of dog all rolled together. Pure mutt!"

"It's awfully young, Cissie," Mrs. Rose said. "It seems queer to me that anybody would give you a dog that ought to be with its mother."

Cissie heard her father's warning cough from where he stood at the back of the pickup with his arms full of grocery bags. "The lady told me the dog's mother got killed by a car."

"That's right, Shirley," Walt Rose said. "The woman has a job with the dentist. She can't stay home and feed the puppy, and she can't take it to his office."

Mrs. Rose sighed. "And I suppose that *I* can feed it when Cissie's at school? Oh, all right. It won't be the first animal I've fed out of an eyedropper or a baby bottle. Cissie, bring it inside the house and help me fix up a box for it so I can keep it with me in the kitchen."

As Cissie's father passed her with the groceries he nodded quickly, and she nodded in return. The story about the dentist's lady had gone over just fine.

Lita drifted back to the porch swing where she'd been reading a movie magazine. She picked it up again but didn't open it as Cissie, followed by Darrell, started across the porch. Lita's blue eyes narrowed as she said, "That's sort of odd, your being given a dog by a lady you hardly know. Maybe there's something wrong with the puppy? I think maybe you should have told the lady you didn't want it. I read your horoscope in the paper this morning. It said that this was a day for Librans to be careful they didn't get into deeper water than they could swim in."

Cissie stopped to permit Darrell to lift Spook's head with a dirty finger and look into the puppy's eyes. Darrell told Lita, "Oh, dry up, Lita. This isn't a it, it's a him, and he's got a name. He's Spook. Spook Rose."

"Children!" exclaimed Lita with a scornful sniff, flopping full-length in the swing and opening the magazine to the article she'd been reading about how her favorite rock star put on eye makeup. She'd fix her eyes that way tonight when she went out with Mark, her steady boyfriend.

Darrell opened the front screen door for Cissie, and she went ahead of him into the living room. Looking into the dog's bright eyes, she whispered, "Welcome home, Spook Rose."

Stopping beside his sister, Darrell said softly, "I hope old Lita ain't right about the puppy, Cissie. You know how she reads those horoscopes and claims to be physic."

Cissie corrected her brother. "You got it backwards, Darrell. What she claims to be is psychic. Lots of times what she says doesn't come true, though."

He nodded, then added, "But sometimes it does. You sure did come by this pup in a funny way, Cissie."

"Darrell, there wasn't anything funny about it," said Cissie, as she went toward the kitchen. She shivered as she thought of what would surely have happened to this pup she already loved if she and her father had not found it. Without its mother to feed and protect it, it wouldn't have lived long at all. Something would surely have got it!

2
Mr. Cameron's Report

After one night of whimpering out of loneliness in the rag-filled box Cissie had made up for him, Spook settled down as part of the Rose family. For the first three days he took warm cow's milk from the eyedropper. Afterward, nestled in Mrs. Rose's lap, he started on a baby bottle. Before long he began to yip in excitement when someone came near him with the bottle.

He grew! Oh, how he grew. Cissie felt that she could see him doing so, and each day on her return from school Spook looked a bit bigger.

He stayed the same pale gray that had earned him his name, but there were reddish hairs in his coat by the time he was six months old. Though she thought of him as "her" dog, Spook was in fact an inside family dog by then. The two female, part-collie dogs who lived outside and who slept in the barn never came farther than the back porch. But because he'd been hand raised in the house, Spook became a house dog. He trailed Mrs. Rose everywhere she went, and when she wasn't home, he trailed Lita.

Lita told Cissie laughingly, "He dogs me, Cissie."

"Well, what do you expect from a dog?" Cissie asked her. Then she said, "I'll try to get him to stick his nose outside more this summer when school's out. He ought to get acquainted with the rest of the animals around here."

Lita stared at Spook, then bent to her work of painting her toenails and said, "You know, he is sure a different-looking dog. He doesn't look like a cocker or poodle or collie or Peke or anything I've ever seen before, Cissie. He must be just what I said he was, eighty-seven kinds of dog mixed up into one."

Cissie had to admit, though she didn't want to, that Spook *was* a different-looking dog. He was a sort of big-chested, spraddle-legged dog, and his head was big and long and oddly shaped. His face came down to a sort of pointed snout, and his sharp ears stood out like gray leather triangles. His eyes were brown dog eyes, but they were sort of squinched shut, as if he were always looking into the sun. Her father told her Spook was the spitting image of the female dog he'd hit on the road. So, even if Spook wasn't a raving beauty as dogs went, he seemed to have bred true to type, whatever that was. Both Spook and his mother were mighty funny looking.

Cissie and her father kept their secret. The old dentist Lita had nicknamed Dr. Fang closed his office and went out of business right after they'd found the puppy. The women who had worked with him had got jobs with other dentists, so there was never any danger that Darrell or Lita or Mrs. Rose would mention Spook to them. At first Cissie and Walt Rose talked about admitting the truth, but they decided against it because it would be hard to explain why they had ever told the white lie. Too, Walt Rose still felt bad about hitting the female, and each time Cissie passed that spot on the road she turned her head away.

Day after day, the first month Spook was with them, she watched the newspaper from town. There were a number of ads for lost dogs. But there was never one about a gray dog with a red collar, a female with a puppy. Try as she could to figure out why the dogs had been there in the desert, Cissie could never come up with anything that made good sense, and neither could her father.

Spook was theirs. He was Cissie's mostly, and she loved him.

He had smart ways about him. He was brave. When he was still very small, one of the biggest of the barn cats, the old tom, sneaked inside the house through the kitchen screen door that had accidentally been left ajar. Instead of running to hide under the stove or sofa, Spook started to yelp and bark. Cissie and Darrell and their mother came from the living room and found Spook standing stiff legged in the middle of the kitchen floor, barking and snarling. The big tomcat was drawn up in a hump like the Halloween cat drawings, glaring and hissing at the pup, but he was not attacking Spook the way he attacked the barn dogs.

Mrs. Rose said, "Why, the cat's twice the size Spook is!" and she clapped her hands to shoo the hissing cat away. "Cissie, that dog seems to be a real scrapper."

Darrell agreed. "He sure is. He eats all the meat scraps in the house."

Cissie ignored her brother's words and said, "Mom, maybe Spook'll be a hunting dog for Dad. Maybe he's part pointer."

"I hope so," Mrs. Rose said, "but so far all he's pointed at is the refrigerator."

"Mom, I'll try to teach him some things this summer when school's out," Cissie promised.

"Fine, you do that. The only thing he's learned is to go stand at the door and bark when he needs to go outside. He *is* housebroken, but that's the most I can say about him."

"He'll be a different dog by the time school starts

again this fall," Cissie answered. "I got a book from the school library on how to teach things to dogs. The librarian said I can keep it out all summer."

"Good luck," commented Lita, who had wandered in to find out what all the barking and hissing was about. Just as Cissie was about to ask her angrily what she meant, the phone out in the hallway rang and Lita ran for it, her long, blond hair streaming out behind her. Then came the happy squeal, "Mark!"

Cissie picked Spook up and leaned against the kitchen counter with him. "Mom, Lita's gotten to be a very painful person lately," she said.

Mrs. Rose replied, "Cissie, be nice to your cousin. Lita hasn't anybody at all except us since her father died in Vietnam, and her mother was killed in that car crash when she was little. Lita is the only link to the one and only sister I ever had. Remember, I haven't got any family, not the way you Roses do. There are lots of them. Do you remember them? Do you remember Stella Jane?"

"Yes, Mom, I remember them. I remember Stella Jane real good."

Cissie left the kitchen with her mother, leaving Darrell looking into the refrigerator for a snack. "Does Dad hear from any of the Roses?" Cissie asked.

"No," her mother said without turning around. "If he had, you'd be the first to know, I suppose.

You pick up the afternoon mail out of the mailbox at the highway when you get off the school bus. Don't you ever look at the envelopes the mail comes in?"

"Yes, I always read what's on the top left-hand corner, Mom. If Cletus or Stella Jane writes to Dad, should I let you know first before I give the letter to Dad?"

"Well, that might give me a little time to pull my wits together for what might be coming, but it would be your father's letter to read, not mine."

"I'm keeping my fingers crossed there won't ever be a letter, aren't you, Mom?"

As Mrs. Rose seated herself on the sofa and Spook jumped up to drape himself over her lap, she said, "You know that I am. We don't talk about it, but I think we all are. So far so good, though. Try to put them out of your mind and have a good time this summer with your puppy before you go into the eighth grade in the fall."

"I'll get a new teacher then, Mom. A man this time, Mr. Cameron. He's black. The kids say he's a neat teacher."

"Black, is he?" Shirley Rose hesitated, then said, "You haven't had a black teacher before, have you?"

"No, Mom."

"What will he be teaching you?"

"English."

"Oh? What have you heard about him, Cissie?"

"Lita and Mark had him when we first came here. They liked him, even though he sure hands out the heavy homework assignments."

"Lita had this black teacher? She never told us about him."

Cissie bit her lower lip. "Oh, Mom, don't get mad. Lita didn't want to tell you and Dad. She was scared you would make a fuss and have her transferred out of his class. She wanted to stay with him."

Mrs. Rose shook her head. "Your dad don't hold with black people much. Remember, he grew up in Arkansas. Lita could have been right about your dad being upset. Why did Lita want to stay with this Mr. Cameron?"

"Because he's a real neat teacher. He makes school interesting. I hear that he works kids hard but they get to liking it. Please don't scold Lita about him. I want to have him, too, even if he is supposed to be strict."

Mrs. Rose laughed as she bent over to pat Spook on the head. "Okay, be in Cameron's class, but don't tell your dad, and I won't either. I won't speak to Lita about him at this late date either. I'm glad to hear your teacher is going to be strict. The best teachers I had always were. I respect a good teacher who demands homework and keeps order."

"That's what everybody says Mr. Cameron does, Mom. Nobody dares to throw erasers around in his room."

* * *

That summer was a memorable one for Cissie Rose. She soon learned she wasn't cut out to be a dog trainer, or maybe Spook wasn't cut out to be a trainable dog.

Following the instructions from the school-library book, she took Spook into the fields behind the house and tried to teach him to heel, to walk on a leash at her side. He wouldn't. Either he surged ahead, dragging her behind him over the buck-thorns, or he'd lag behind her so she had to drag him. She tried to teach him to stay on command as the book said, but after a moment he'd come up to her as if he'd never heard the word. He didn't sit any better than he heeled or stayed. He didn't learn roll over or dead dog either, and she didn't have the heart to scold him.

Spook did not understand what Cissie was trying to teach him because she went about it incorrectly. He was confused by her new behavior, so different from her former way of treating him. She put a collar around his neck, something he'd never had to wear before. It made his neck itch. And then she tied a line to the collar and jerked him about by it. He didn't like the leash, and he didn't know what Cissie wanted him to do. He'd rather run free with her the way they'd done before.

First she scowled at him and scolded him, shaking her finger when he disobeyed. The next moment she was laughing at him and hugging him when he did the exact same wrong thing. He had no way of knowing what this girl he loved wanted, because she didn't give him the right instructions. He didn't know that her book on dogs said she was to be very firm with the dog at all times while the training was going on. Cissie couldn't be firm at all times, though, so she'd laugh and show him affection when she should not have. The end of the training sessions always came as a relief to Spook. He barked wildly and dashed about joyously, circling Cissie the moment she unsnapped the leash from his collar.

By summer's end, Cissie knew quite a bit about dog training, but Spook didn't seem to know anything. She decided that he needed to go to obedience school where he'd be trained by an expert among other dogs. Training a dog when you really didn't know what you were doing only ended up in not training him at all.

The one thing she learned was that he wasn't afraid of anything that moved! Spook squared off against their Guernsey cow, who came up once to sniff at him in curiosity. His snarls and barks drove her to the far end of her pasture, where she stopped to look accusingly at him over her shoulder. He attacked the barn's big tomcat in the front yard, and this time got badly scratched along the side of his head, but that didn't teach him not to tangle with the tom. Every time he saw the cat he was ready to do battle and had to be hauled away by Cissie or Darrell. Spook crawled under a barbed-wire fence to confront the big cream-colored Nubian goat Darrell was raising to show at the county fair. The goat made four butting runs at the dodging Spook before Darrell and Cissie, attracted by the goat's bleating, got Spook out of its pen.

Walt and Shirley Rose looked on with amusement, but they were secretly impressed with Cissie's refusal to give up and admit that her dog wasn't going to learn.

The night before Cissie, Darrell, and Lita started back to school for the autumn term, Walt Rose told his wife privately, "Well, Shirley, whatever we know about Cissie's dog, he seems to be a fine watchdog for the house. He'll be good company for you here when I'm away in town seeing old Mr. Benson."

She laughed and said, "Yes, Spook's company, all right. My only company most of the time. He even keeps the poor cats from coming up to the back porch for their kitchen scraps. It's a good thing door-to-door salesmen don't come all the way out here. Spook wouldn't take one bit to strangers!"

Walt Rose nodded. "No, I don't suppose he would. That's all right with me. It'd be different if we lived in town where there are always other folks close by. It's good to have a dog who means business way out here, Shirley."

The Staffordshire Terror

* * *

After the first week in her new class, Cissie decided that her black teacher Mr. Cameron was just as neat as Lita had said he was. He was young and wore nice clothes, not jeans and shirts, but pants and coats that matched. Sometimes he even wore vests, fancy ones made out of velvet that he told his admiring girl students, when they asked, were made by his fiancée.

He taught English to Cissie first period in the morning, and at the end of the day she and the other pupils in his homeroom came back to be counted before they went out to the waiting school buses. He sometimes made jokes about how surprised he was to find the same number of kids in the afternoon as in the morning. He said it amazed him that they found their way safe and sound each day across the battlefields of the middle school to his room and arrived alive and unwounded.

There wasn't one bit of uproar in his classes and very little whispering either. He was a tough teacher, but he never tongue-lashed kids for reading out loud poorly or because they had trouble with nouns and verbs. As far as she was concerned he had only one real fault, which she'd been warned about. He was crazy on the subject of homework. He loved written reports. It didn't matter what a kid wrote about—a vacation, a trip, a hobby—or whether the kid wrote a short story, an essay, or even a poem.

Cissie was faced with so many choices for her first report that she couldn't make up her mind what to write about. Two weeks before the report was due, she took up the problem with her family after supper.

"What'll I write about?"

Lita gave her the answer as she cleared off the table. "That animal!"

"Which one?" asked Darrell.

With the fork in her hand Lita pointed at Spook, who was sitting beside Cissie's chair, hoping to be fed something tasty from her plate. "That one down there. That dog."

Cissie demanded angrily, "What would I say about him? Why are you picking on Spook, Lita?"

Lita picked up a dirty plate. "Well, you can hardly write about how smart and well behaved he is, can you?"

Darrell got in on the joke, too. "Or how well trained he is."

"Well, what then?" flared Cissie.

Lita went on smoothly. "Write about what *kind* of dog he is. Look up what kind of mutt that lady at the dentist's office palmed off on you. Look it up in the encyclopedia."

Cissie's mother said quickly to keep the peace,

"That's a good idea, Cissie. Maybe your dog isn't a pure mutt. Maybe he's half something, or maybe he's a whole something."

Cissie frowned, then said, "I suppose I could try to do that."

Lita stopped in the doorway with a pile of dishes. "I've got another idea, one that'll get you an *A* I bet. Mark's coming over tonight with the camera he got for his birthday. It's the kind that takes pictures on the spot. I'll ask him to take one of Spook, so you can paste that to your report, Cissie."

"That'd be good," said Darrell. "That way, Cissie, even if you can't find out what kind of dog Spook is, you can let Mr. Cameron know what Spook looks like."

"Would Mr. Cameron really like a picture?" Cissie asked Lita.

"I suspect he would," said Lita. "But ask the school librarian for help. We do that all the time in high school when we have to do reports."

As Lita went out of the room, Mrs. Rose said, "It's going to be dark by the time Mark gets here, Cissie. He'll need to use that flash thing in the camera, so I suppose you'll have to hold Spook, and Darrell will have to hang on to him, too. That flash will startle the dog."

"Does that mean we get to be in the picture, too?" Darrell asked, sounding pleased.

Cissie told her brother, "I bet Mark can take it so

our heads don't show at all, only our hands holding Spook's collar." She laughed, and Darrell made a face at her.

The resulting picture was a queer one. It showed only Cissie's and Darrell's hands, feet, and knees as they knelt on each side of the dog, but it showed Spook just fine. He was glaring into the camera, and his eyes glowed bright red on the color print Mark hauled out a minute later. The flash had made the dog jump and pull free from the children.

"He looks great," exclaimed Cissie.

Lita, however, looking over her shoulder, muttered, "Only a mother could love a face like that, and to think he was sort of a cute puppy!"

Cissie kept the snapshot in her arithmetic book and showed it to no one but the school librarian, a tall, soft-voiced, blond woman.

"Hmmm," she murmured, "this certainly isn't any everyday dog, is it? We have a special one-volume dog encyclopedia here. I suggest you look in that instead of in the regular encyclopedias for a start. It might be quicker for you. Look through the photographs of dog breeds page by page. Then, if you see a dog that resembles yours, look it up under the name of the breed."

"Thank you."

The dog encyclopedia was heavy, big, and red, and it had hundreds of pages. It was full of dog photographs and drawings, page after page of them. Cissie looked at collies, spaniels of several kinds, Dobermans, Boxers, Samoyeds, Malamutes, Chihuahuas, dachshunds, poodles, Pekingese, and breeds so strange she couldn't pronounce their names.

At last she got to the section on terriers. There, near the last page of that section, she found a side view picture of a dog that looked like Spook. It was black and white, but its head looked like Spook's. On the next page there was a front view of the dog, and it looked even more like Spook. The dog had the same bowed-out front legs and big chest and pointy ears. Under both photographs were the words, *Staffordshire terrier.*

Cissie excitedly read the entry that told her Staffordshire terriers were an old breed from England and named for a county there. They were originally a cross between a terrier and a bulldog, and they were often called bullterriers. Another name for them was "pit bull," because hundreds of years ago they'd fought other dogs in pits, places in theaters, where men could stand over the fighting dogs and bet on which dog would win. Sometimes these dogs were entered in pairs to harry a bull or a captive bear by grabbing him by the muzzle.

Cissie's eyes grew wider as she stared at the page in front of her, remembering how Spook had acted around the cow and the goat. She thought of the name on the red collar Spook's mother had worn, and she read through the rest of the section looking at the long, fancy names that belonged to the famous dogs in the pictures. But she couldn't find either Fame or Folly mentioned anywhere.

Taking a pencil out of her pencil box and a sheet of paper from her notebook, Cissie scribbled down facts for her report. Then she returned the encyclopedia to the librarian, thanked her, and left the library.

Cissie didn't tell her news to Darrell on the bus back home or to anyone else until after supper. She waited until Lita had finished her dessert; then she took a deep breath and said, "Lita, I have something to tell you. Spook isn't just any old dog the way you think he is." Cissie fondled Spook's ears as she made her announcement.

"What kind is he? A nothing but a hound dog?" asked Lita, laughing.

"No, he's a Staffordshire terrier. That's a dog from England. It's an old-time fighting dog."

Mrs. Rose asked, "He's a purebred dog then?"

"Yes, he is, Mom."

Walt Rose said, laughing, "Well, he did take on the cow and the goat, and they're a mite bigger than he is."

"And the old tomcat, too, over and over!" added Darrell.

That night, while Cissie sat alone looking at the

stars with Spook at her feet in the porch swing, her father came out to sit beside her.

After a time of swinging together, he said, "Cissie, what you found out today might have explained why Spook's mother didn't get out of the way of my pickup. Maybe it wasn't in her nature to run, to move away from anything. Maybe she'd never seen a car coming toward her before."

"Maybe not, Dad. Maybe she was raised different from other dogs. I didn't forget about her collar. I looked up the words on her collar in the dog book, but they weren't there. Anyway, Spook's a Staffordshire terrier for sure, and he's plenty special."

Cissie's report got an *A* from Mr. Cameron, who read it aloud to his English class. She said in it that she got the dog as a present, sticking to the story she'd made up with her dad. Then she went on to write that Spook would fight anything at any time but wasn't any great shakes as a well-trained dog.

At the end of the report Mr. Cameron chuckled and told his class, "This sounds like quite a dog. But the dog's taste for fighting doesn't sound good to me. It isn't right to be eager to fight all the time. Even men who are boxers don't fight all the time."

The boy at the desk across from Cissie whispered loud enough for everybody to hear, "Mr. Cameron was a boxer."

Cameron heard him. "That's right. I used to be.

I fought in the Navy and afterward for a time. But you don't see me fighting now. There's no point in it unless you have to. That's one of the big differences between a man and an animal. Do you see that, Cissie? You ought to work hard to train your dog. You sound proud of his liking to fight, but you'll be prouder if you teach him how to behave someday."

Cissie held up her hand, then stood up to say, "But that's all Spook can do so far is fight!"

Everybody laughed, and she sat down with a burning face. But she had got the only *A* in the class for her report. At least that grade proved that Spook was interesting, and he was a lot more special than she'd thought. Nobody in her class but Mr. Cameron had ever heard of Staffordshire terriers, and he said he'd only read about them.

A month went by. During that time Spook gained three pounds. Lita broke up with Mark and went back to Mark, and Cissie made a report on the mockingbirds that had nested in the tree just outside her bedroom window. Her dad's employer, Mr. Benson, came out from Riverside to inspect the place. He said he was satisfied with the way the Roses kept it and went back to town. He never even saw Spook. Cissie locked him inside her bedroom with her and kept him quiet while Benson was there. Mr. Benson wouldn't care that they had another dog, but she wasn't sure how Spook would take to him, and she was afraid he might snarl and make Mr. Benson mad. After all, Benson owned the little ranch.

Toward the end of the month, on the last Saturday, the Roses had unexpected company.

Cissie and Darrell, who had walked out to the main road to the mailbox, saw the old black sedan slow down in front of them, make the turn into their private road, and stop.

Darrell's hand brushed Cissie's arm. Then he said hurriedly under his breath, "Oh, my gosh, it's *them*! He's found us."

With the daily newspaper and a letter for her mother in one hand, Cissie turned around after closing the mailbox. She stared at the car first, seeing the pale, red-haired girl and, beyond the girl, the head of the man who was the driver.

"It's Uncle Cletus!" Cissie exclaimed softly to her brother. "Oh, Lordy, we got troubles again. It's him and Stella Jane. They tracked us down."

3
The Bad Brother

"Hop in, kids. There's room," ordered Cletus Rose without getting out from behind the wheel.

Cissie walked slowly around to the side of his old car, but not Darrell, who stayed put. Her father's oldest brother hadn't changed much since she'd last seen him in Washington State. His hair was grayer now under his straw cowboy-style hat, and he was heavier, but his face was as broad and shiny red as ever.

Uncle Cletus and Walt Rose had owned a little radiator repair shop together in Washington as they had in Texas and before that in Arkansas, where Cissie had been born. In all three states Cletus had written checks when he knew he didn't have enough money in the bank to cover them. Because Dad had been his partner in the business, folks they owed money to naturally expected her dad to make the checks good. She knew that her uncle had never bothered to tell her dad what sort of crooked thing he was up to until the very last minute. Then he'd come around and say that he was getting out of town "right now and if you're smart, Walt, you'll pull up stakes, too."

Finally Dad had enlisted in the U.S. Army up in Washington State and gone overseas at once. That had been a lonesome time for all of them, and her mom had acted sort of queer, quiet and sad, writing him letters and getting letters from him where she worked because they kept moving from apartment to apartment. Mom didn't talk about them or him except to say Dad was okay and sent his love.

Cissie detested her Uncle Cletus, her dad's "bad brother," and she was sorry for poor, silent Stella Jane, his daughter.

Once more Cletus ordered Cissie, "Get in the car, kid."

But Cissie shook her head and fibbed fast, "We're waiting out here for somebody to come by with a package for Mom." Then she added, "Hello, Stella Jane. How are you?"

"All right, Cissie," Stella Jane said softly with a wan little smile.

Cissie asked her, not her father, "Stella Jane, how did you know where we were?"

But Stella Jane didn't get a chance to answer.

42

Cletus guffawed with laughter and waggled a thick finger at Cissie. "Your mama sent a Christmas card to some of the family back in Arkansas, and they sent me your address down here in California. So after a time I felt like movin' out of Idaho because of the cold winters, and we packed up and drove down here to see you folks, my family. See you at the house, kids." He stepped on the gas and started down the dirt road, raising clouds of yellow dust.

Cissie and Darrell stared after the car. After a time she said, "I sure hope he doesn't plan to settle around here, but I bet he does. Whatever he does I'm scared we'll be stuck with him for house company for a couple of days. Mom won't like that. Dad either."

Darrell said, as he looked at the dust ahead of them, "We coulda rode home with him and Stella Jane."

"No! I don't want to have any more of him than I have to, Darrell. I wish Spook'd scare him off our property, but Dad'll see to it that he doesn't. Dad wouldn't sic my dog onto his own brother."

"Will this mean we have to move again?" asked Darrell.

"I hope not. I sure hope not."

Spook was lolling, head on his paws, on the front porch when he heard the sounds of the strange car approaching. He got to his feet and came to the top of the steps, then let out a series of sharp barks. The barking brought Walt Rose out of the barn to the yard and Shirley Rose out of the house onto the porch, where both of them waited together beside the terrier.

"Oh, my Lord!" came the soft wail from Mrs. Rose, who was first to recognize the passengers in the black car. "It's Cletus and Stella Jane, Walt."

Mr. Rose didn't say anything, but he stiffened and put his balled fists into the pockets of his overalls.

Spook sensed their tension as the auto came into the space between the barn and the house. His hackles started to rise, and a growl began in his chest.

"What'll we do, Walt?" asked Mrs. Rose.

"Nothing right now, Shirley. There ain't no call to create trouble if we don't have to. Let's see how Cletus behaves. There's no cause to rile him. Remember, all we want here is some peace for a change."

Mrs. Rose muttered bitterly, "With your brother anywhere nearby, there won't be any real peace." She reached down and patted Spook on the shoulder.

He stopped growling, but his hackles didn't go down. His eyes were fixed on the car, watching it as he watched all strange cars. The fear he scented from the people with him made him warier than usual.

The car stopped and a man got out. He waved his hat and called out, "Hey, Walt, it's me, your big brother, Cletus. How are y'all? I got Stella Jane here with me."

"Hello, Cletus," called Walt Rose, who hadn't moved.

Spook tensed as the strange man came toward the porch. The dog lifted his head to get his smell. Cletus smelled of sweat, oil, onions, and something rank and sweetish, the odor of whiskey, though Spook didn't know it. The dog didn't like the smell, and he didn't like the tension in the air or the fear scents of his family behind him. His growl came again, and he bared his teeth. He came nearer to the top step and crouched.

"Walt, the dog!" said Mrs. Rose in a whisper.

"Hey, Walt, where'd you get that hound?" shouted Cletus, ten or so feet from the porch.

Walt Rose didn't answer and didn't move. He looked down at Spook, and he grinned. He waited while Spook went on growling. "He don't like you, Cletus," he called out at last. Then he reached down and got the dog by the collar. "Simmer down, Spook," he told him. "It's only my brother. Don't you move, Cletus, till I got the dog under control."

Spook went on growling while a narrow-eyed

Cletus stood motionless. Then Walt Rose said, "Shirley, you'd better put Spook in the tool shed so Cletus and Stella Jane can come inside."

"All right, Walt."

Spook felt the hand of Cissie's mother on his collar. Her words were soft. "Come on, Spook! Good dog! Good dog!"

The next three days were strained ones for Cissie and her family.

Because she pitied her, Cissie tried once to talk to Stella Jane out in the kitchen. It wasn't worth the effort, though Cissie felt better for having tried.

First she asked her how she'd liked Idaho's climate and weather. Stella Jane looked even more mournful than usual and said, "Well, the winters do get awful cold, and there's a lot of snow there."

"Did you have a job there?"

"No, Pa said he didn't want me working and picking up with the wrong sort of folks."

"With all that snow around did you go skiing?"

"No." Stella Jane looked away from Cissie and added, "Pa went hunting, though, and fishing, too. There are deer up there. Lots of them. He always got some venison to put in the freezer. He took me out fishing once."

"What was that like?" Cissie asked.

Stella Jane shrugged her shoulders. "Okay, I

guess, but the mosquitoes were bad. We rented a boat and went out lake fishing. I rowed while Pa stood up, fly-casting. I'd never rowed before and wasn't very good. The oars splashed too much and scared the trout away."

Cissie nodded. "I never rowed a boat either."

"It isn't as easy as it looks," Stella Jane volunteered. "It takes practice."

Cissie decided to change the subject. "What kind of place did you live in up there?"

"We rented a little house in town. It was sort of cute. There was a big weeping willow tree in the front yard. It was pretty as could be." Stella Jane sighed.

"Did you like Idaho?" asked Cissie.

"Yes. It was the nicest place I've lived in yet."

Unnoticed by Stella Jane, Cissie shook her head. Idaho didn't sound so nice to her, but then no place with Uncle Cletus would be nice to her way of thinking.

With his dog instincts, Spook took an immediate dislike to Cletus. Cissie thought it would be great to have a smeller like a dog's that would let you know right off, with one whiff, who was a bad person. After Cissie coaxed Spook awhile, he tolerated the company of Stella Jane, but he never got used to Cletus. All the time that Cletus was with them, Cissie had to tie the terrier in the shed so he couldn't growl at him. When Cissie wasn't at school, she was out in the shed with Spook and often with Darrell, who came there, too.

The afternoon of the third day of Cletus's and Stella Jane's visit, Lita also came out and sat down on top of a paint storage chest to pat Spook. Her pretty face was close to tears.

"I take back everything I ever said about your dog," she told Cissie. "He's got brains all right. I hear that he figured out old Cletus right away. Oh, but I just hate old Cletus!" Lita exploded angrily. "He's in there right now with a bottle of beer talking about what a big, important man he is and how much money he made last year betting on horse races. I wish your dad would throw him out."

Darrell said, "Uncle Cletus is bigger'n Dad is."

Lita shook her head. "That isn't why he doesn't. Your uncle has something on your dad, maybe something he could get in trouble for."

"Dad never did anything wrong," flared Cissie.

Lita bit at a fingernail. "It's hard to believe, but Stella Jane and I had a talk real early this morning before anyone else was awake. Maybe it's a good thing we're in the same bedroom." Lita sighed. "Poor Stella Jane. Her mother's been dead, too, a lot longer than mine has. Stella Jane hardly remembers her at all. I think it was because I got to talking about Mark that Stella Jane finally opened up. When she started, I couldn't have stopped her if I wanted to. She sure is a mess, and I know why."

"Why?" asked Cissie, going to sit beside Spook and tenderly laying her head alongside his. How sorry she felt for thin, shy, white-faced Stella Jane, who never spoke above a whisper and who seemed to get smaller when her father spoke to her.

"She's scared of her dad," Lita continued. "She says he's got a horrible temper. She's afraid to speak out in front of him for fear of saying something that'd make him mad. She didn't want to leave Idaho. Her boyfriend up there wanted to marry her."

"She had a *boyfriend?*" Cissie asked in surprise. Then she giggled and said, "Hey, that's why she liked Idaho, I bet."

"I guess it must be. Well, the boyfriend sells real estate there, and he told Cletus he wanted to marry Stella Jane. Cletus told him no and punched him in the face, and then Cletus packed Stella Jane and himself up and came down here right off. Stella Jane's boyfriend doesn't even know where she is."

"Oh, golly!" Cissie sat up straight, while Darrell made a hissing sound.

"That isn't all. Stella Jane said that her dad is going to set up a car-repair shop in Riverside. He told her if she dares to get in touch with her boyfriend in Idaho, he'll make her sorry and him too. So Stella Jane's got to keep house for the mean old geezer. She says he won't let her go to work where she can meet any folks. She's scared to write her boyfriend for fear Cletus would get hold of one of the boyfriend's letters to her somehow. He'd go crazy mad. She's his prisoner the way her mom was."

"No wonder she looks sad and doesn't talk!" Cissie exclaimed.

"Yes. Just living with that old Cletus would make a person look sad," agreed Lita.

"I'm getting madder and madder at our uncle," Cissie said. "I hate keeping my dog out here where he's lonesome when we're away."

"You know, I miss old Spook being around, too," said Lita. "He sort of grows on a person. Well, I know for a fact that Stella Jane and her dad won't be here much longer. Stella Jane told me this morning. They're going to Riverside tomorrow and rent a place to live in."

"Good. Then all we have to do is put up with him for another supper, and that'll be the last one!"

"It won't be good, you can bet on that," said Lita grimly. "Boy, it's hard for me even to look at him and watch him eat. His table manners are the worst I've ever seen."

That supper was the most dreadful Cissie had ever experienced. Lita had been absolutely right, and Lita's disliking Cletus had brought them closer than before. Rather than look at her uncle, Cissie often looked across the table at Lita, who kept her eyes fixed on her plate most of the time.

Cletus Rose was full of food and even fuller of beer by dessert time. He got off onto the subject of horses and dogs the Rose family had owned back in Arkansas when he and Walt had been boys. He talked about how fast the horses had been in those days and how good the family dogs had been at coon hunting. Suddenly he asked Walt, "Do you remember old Heller and what a good scrapping dog he was?"

"Yep, Cletus, but that was a long time back."

Cletus lit a cigar and said, "That gray animal I seen when I first come here looks to me to be worth something, Walt."

Cissie sat up straighter than ever now. Her father said, "He's Cissie's dog, Cletus."

Her uncle swung his big head to look at her. "Your dog, huh? He's a lot of dog for a kid like you to have. How'd you come by him, missy?"

Cissie replied stiffly. "A lady gave him to me. He's a Staffordshire terrier."

Darrell added, "Cissie wrote a report at school about her dog. She got a *A* on it. She found out that Spook comes from a lot of fighting dogs over in England. They're real fancy dogs."

"That's mighty interesting, ain't it? There ain't much to fight out here, is there?" Cletus grinned and reached for his beer. "I used to know a man who trained young fighting dogs in his barn. He used to lower yowling kittens in onion sacks from the rafters and tease the pup by jerking the sack up just before the pup could get to it. His dogs got so danged mad that they'd run after anything."

"That's horrible," cried Shirley Rose.

Cletus grinned at her. "Oh, it got worse. Sometimes he let the cat all the way down."

Cissie, who had listened in horror with her hand to her mouth, leaped up and fled out of the room. Lita followed right after her.

Cletus roared with laughter and then shouted, "What's the matter with your gal, Walt, and Miss High-and-Mighty-Yellow-Hair? Don't they like what I said?"

"You said enough for now, Cletus," warned Walt Rose.

"Pa, please," came from Stella Jane's soft voice.

"You shut up, Stella Jane," boomed the man. "I say what I want to say. Nobody can tell me what—"

Shirley Rose's voice cut sharply across Cletus's words. "Darrell, leave the table. Stella Jane, please help me get the dishes into the kitchen."

"Ah, go on. Go ahead, Stella Jane," ordered Cletus, when his daughter looked to him for permission.

Cissie had gone only as far as the hallway. She

stood there, leaning against the wall, her eyes closed. The vision of the terrified kitten in the mesh bag and of the dog waiting below made her feel sick to her stomach. It was different when Spook chased the barn tomcat, because the tom could always get away from him. But a poor little kitten in a sack!

"Cissie, Cissie." She felt Lita's arm about her shoulders. Cissie opened her eyes and saw that her cousin's were sparkling with rage. "Cissie, *that did it*! What he said just now finally did it! I'm going to do something to that old Cletus."

"What'll you do?" Cissie asked.

Lita pulled her close and held her. "I think I know a way to put a spoke in his wheel. I'm going to get the name and address of Stella Jane's boyfriend. I'm going to write him and let him know where she is now. And I'll keep it a secret from everybody but you. I bet he writes back to me, and I'll let her know what he says. Cissie, you pick up the mail in the box on the road. Will you help me and keep it secret, too?"

"Sure, Lita. You bet I will! I sure hated Uncle Cletus just now when he was talking about those poor cats."

"We'll pay him back, Cissie. If we need help, Mark'll help Stella Jane, too. I know he will. Mark will help us out whenever we need him."

"Oh, Lita!" Cissie flung her arms around the

smart-aleck cousin she sometimes got mad at. Lita was on the side of the Roses every bit as much as Darrell was.

Just as Stella Jane had said, she and Cletus left for town the next morning. Their old black sedan passed Cissie, Lita, and Darrell on their way up the road to the school bus.

Stella Jane smiled, then waved.

Lita whispered to Cissie, "I told Stella Jane that I'd try to get in touch with her boyfriend for her and let her know when I do. She cried, she was so happy."

Darrell demanded, "What are you girls whispering about?"

"Important stuff," Cissie replied. "Secret stuff." She asked Lita, "Did Stella Jane think they'd have trouble finding a place to live in town?"

"No, her dad had her look in the newspaper for places for rent. She said there were scads of them in Riverside."

"That's too bad," said Darrell. Then he added, "You know, I saw Uncle Cletus by the tool shed real early this morning. He was looking through the window. I bet he was looking at Spook."

Cissie chuckled. "And I bet Spook was looking back at him, growling. Well, Mom can let my dog out now. And it's about time, too. I'm sure glad Dad isn't going into the repair-shop business with him or any other kind of business either. I asked Mom about that just before I went up to bed. She said Dad had promised her he wouldn't. He'd keep on working for Mr. Benson. So I guess we don't have to worry about leaving here."

"Nope, I guess we don't." Darrell was walking on the high crown of the one-lane road. "Dad and Uncle Cletus were talking out in the barn last night. I saw 'em. Dad was showing Uncle Cletus something that looked like an old dog collar. It was a red one."

Cissie drew in her breath. "What did they say about it? Did you hear?"

"Yes. Dad said he found the collar on the main road last year, and he wondered if Uncle Cletus might know about the words that were on it."

"What did Uncle Cletus say?"

"He said it was a fancy collar and the kind rich people's dogs wore. He said some parts of it were real silver. Dad said that soon as Spook was all the way big enough, he might put the collar on him."

"No!" burst out Cissie. "Spook'll have a nice collar of his own. Not some other dog's!" To herself she thought, Not one that belonged to a dog that's dead.

Her dad had been trying to find out something about Spook's mother. She was glad that Uncle Cletus hadn't known about the words on the collar. Somehow his interest in Spook made her uneasy.

Lita wrote secretly that very evening to Stella Jane's boyfriend, and the next morning on the way to the school bus she stuffed her letter into the Rose's mailbox, telling Darrell she was sending away for some sample colognes. The wink she gave Cissie made clear what the letter truly was, and Cissie winked in return.

Two months went by. Cissie reckoned that Spook was a year old now. Though he had his growth, he still showed some puppy ways, such as liking to climb up on her lap while she watched television. He was pretty big for that, and his weight made her thighs ache sometimes, but she didn't have the heart to push him off because then he looked so sad and wounded. He made a laughable picture, lying across her with his head hanging over one side and his back legs and tail on Darrell or Lita or whoever sat next to her on the sofa.

Those were quiet months. Uncle Cletus didn't come visiting, and he didn't call on the telephone either. He didn't invite Walt Rose or his family to the apartment he and Stella Jane had rented on Fourth Street. Stella Jane was the one who kept in touch with the family, talking once a week to Mrs. Rose and more often to Lita.

Once Cissie heard her mother ask, "What do you and Stella Jane talk about for such a long time? You talked for a full hour last night. You and she are as different as day and night, and she's six years older than you are. In all the years I've known Stella Jane I've never heard her say more than two sentences at a time. What does she say to you?" Cissie's mother put down the knife she was using to peel apples and looked at Lita. "Lita, is her father giving her a hard time?"

Lita, who was peeling fruit for pies along with Cissie and Mrs. Rose, said, "No, Aunt Shirley. She says old Cletus is busy all the time getting his business started at the new repair shop. He's there all the time."

"But what do you talk about?"

Cissie felt Lita's foot touch her ankle gently under the kitchen table, but it wasn't necessary. Cissie knew what they talked about. She'd taken the four letters from Idaho out of the mailbox and given them secretly to Lita, telling Darrell that they were from advertisers and TV stars Lita wrote to. She knew that Lita read the boyfriend's letters—his name was Mr. Redpath—aloud over the phone to Stella Jane when nobody else was near the hallway. Then, in turn, Stella Jane told Lita what to write back. It was all very exciting, Cisse thought.

Lita answered her aunt. "Stella Jane's taken up sewing. We talk about what she's making, and then I talk about what I'm doing in high school and about what Mark and I are doing. Mark and I drive up and down Magnolia Street in town for hours every Saturday night. Even if she's older than we are, I wish we could go get Stella Jane some night and take her with us."

"Lita, you'd better not," warned Mrs. Rose.

"I know that. Mark and I won't go near Stella Jane."

Cissie's mother sighed. "I wish there was some way to rescue that poor girl from Cletus, so she could have some sort of life of her own."

Once more Lita kicked Cissie under the table. Cissie went on peeling her apple and said nothing.

Two weeks later Cletus Rose came down the private road to his brother's place. He came without warning, without calling, and he came after nine o'clock at night. Cissie saw the headlights of his car, dipping and lifting, as he drove at high speed along the bumpy road. The night was warm, and her window was open. She went to it and leaned out over the sill, aware that Lita was doing the same thing at the next window.

"It isn't Mark," said Lita. "He's playing in a basketball game in Redlands tonight."

The girls looked on while the car came to a rocking halt in front of the house. It was a light-colored sedan they'd never seen before, and Cissie didn't recognize the driver until he hurtled out of the front seat.

"Uncle Cletus!" she said under her breath. Then

58

she headed for the stairs, because already she could hear Spook barking from inside the living room. The barn dogs were barking, too.

She ran downstairs to the front door and caught Spook by his collar. She told her mother and father, who'd come from the back porch where they'd been stacking some canned goods, "It's Uncle Cletus! I saw him."

"Cissie, get your dog upstairs!" Walt Rose ordered.

Cissie struggled with Spook, hauling him backward, while Cletus Rose banged on the front door with his fist.

"He's sure angry about something, Walt!" warned Mrs. Rose.

Finally Cissie managed to get the plunging Spook turned around, and she dragged him through the living room into the hall and halfway up the stairs where she paused, out of breath.

Her uncle went on banging until her father unbolted the door he always bolted at nine o'clock. Holding tight to the dog, Cissie sat down on the stairs. She was aware that Lita and Darrell were standing together at the top.

No one could miss hearing Cletus; he was yelling so. His first words were, "Stella Jane's run off with that guy from Idaho!"

"What guy?" they heard Walt Rose asking.

The reply was a shouted one. "The one she was

messing around with when we were living in Poca-
tello, the real-estate salesman. He courted her behind my back while I was working my tail off in
my shop. He drove down here and got her. While
I was working here he come to our place, and she
packed up and run off with him to get married."

A small, joyful gasp burst from Lita at the top
of the stairs. A grin spread over Cissie's face. Good
for Stella Jane!

Cissie heard her dad ask, "How do you know
that Stella Jane ran off?"

"She left me a note on the kitchen table." Cletus
was still shouting. "I ain't as dumb as you think I
am. What I want to know is how this guy from
Idaho knew where Stella Jane was?"

Cissie's mother said, "Maybe Stella Jane wrote
him a letter, or maybe she called him on the telephone."

Cletus bawled at Shirley Rose, "That ain't it.
She'd be too scared. Somebody fixed it up for her."

"Well, Cletus, we certainly didn't do that," said
Mrs. Rose.

Cissie heard Lita moving down the stairs behind
her until she was standing on the step just above
her and Spook.

Cletus shouted, "Maybe you and Walt didn't,
Shirley, but somebody else here could have done it."

"You mean one of my kids, Cletus!" Cissie's dad

sounded as if he couldn't believe what he'd just heard.

"Nope, Walt. Not them. I mean your wife's relation, Miss High-and-Mighty, the yellow-headed, long-haired one. I know for a fact that Stella Jane used to talk to her on the telephone."

"*Lita?*" asked Mrs. Rose.

"You bet. Lita. Yeah, she's the one I mean."

"Lita hasn't made any phone calls to Idaho, Cletus," Mrs. Rose told him calmly. "I see the phone bill here, and so does Walt."

"There's other ways of meddling in my business."

Suddenly Lita said, "Let me by, Cissie."

"*No! Don't!*" Cissie didn't move. She reached up to catch at Lita's bathrobe and stop her, but Lita pushed by her and Spook and headed straight for the living room.

Holding tight to Spook's collar, Cissie followed Lita, and Darrell brought up the rear.

Cissie watched Lita sail into the living room with her head high. In her white bathrobe she looked like a princess. Lita stopped a distance from the scarlet-faced Cletus and announced, "I heard everything you said down here. *I* fixed it for Stella Jane! You bet I did! She gave me her fiancé's name and address, and I wrote to him for her. I did it all with letters."

"*Lita!*" cried Mrs. Rose.

61

"I knew it. I knew who did it. I'll git—" bellowed Cletus, choking wth anger as he shook a fist at Lita.

"*Cletus!*" Walt Rose shouted.

"I'm goin' to take care of you right now, you. . . ." Cletus took a step forward toward Lita.

Cissie's cry rang out over the room from where she stood in the doorway. "Shall I let go of my dog?"

"*No! Hold him!*" shouted her father.

Excited by all the noise and by the threatening gestures of this man with the smell he hated, the terrier was jerking forward, trying to free himself and attack Cletus.

"Get out of here, Cletus!" Walt Rose cried to his brother. "Get out right now. *Hurry!*"

Cissie took her eyes from Spook and saw Cletus staring at her, not Lita now, and that he had lowered his fist. He took a step backward.

"I can't hold him much longer, Dad!" shouted Cissie. Each lunge Spook made was stronger.

All at once Cletus Rose spun on his heel, went out the door, and slammed it behind him.

Cissie let the dog go. Spook ran, digging his claws into the carpet, crumpling it, leaping against the door. He thudded into it, fell back, then began scratching at it, trying to get at the man on the front porch.

"You ain't heard the last of this!" thundered Cletus from the window, shaking his fist. Then, as

62

Cissie got the terrier by the collar again, they heard Cletus stomp down the steps and a moment later start the engine of his new car and drive off.

"Oh, wow!" Lita said. And she went to sit on the sofa and put her head into her hands.

The Rose family looked at her, then at the front door, and finally at Spook, who was still growling.

"Well," was Mrs. Rose's only comment, and she sat down, too, next to Lita. "You sure took a lot on yourself, Lita," she said, patting Lita's shoulder.

Cissie cried, "I knew about it, too, Mom! We wanted to help Stella Jane. It wasn't only Lita. It was me, too. Don't be mad at us!"

"I'm not mad," said Walt Rose. "I'm sort of glad Stella Jane got away. Lita and Cissie, you did just fine."

But Mrs. Rose was shaking her head. "Walt, what happened here just now won't make your brother one bit friendly to us now. You know how he is." She turned to Lita. "You've got yourself a real enemy, Lita, somebody to look out for. We all have."

Darrell piped up, "Uncle Cletus don't know about Cissie knowing, though." He pointed to his sister. "Now I know what all that whispering was about and what was in those letters you put in and took out of the mailbox. Next time you're up to something, let me in on it too!"

Cissie asked her father, "Dad, will Uncle Cletus try to get even with Lita?"

Walt Rose sighed. "Probably. He won't stop at Lita, though. It'll be all of us now. He might have stopped at Lita, who ain't a Rose by birth, if it hadn't been for the dog, Cissie. In time I mighta talked Cletus out of being so mad at Lita by pointing out to him that somebody else is supporting his daughter now. But when you showed up with Spook, things got taken out of my hands fast. Cletus won't remember that we kept the dog off him tonight. He'll sulk about losing Stella Jane because of what Lita did, and he'll remember the dog hitting the front door just after he left. There's no telling what he'll do, but it will be something we won't like at all. He has it in for your dog now, too!"

Cissie scoffed, "Spook can take care of himself!"

4
Miranda

Cletus Rose drove to his apartment on Fourth Street, went to the refrigerator, and took out three cans of beer. Then he sat down in front of the TV. He didn't turn the set on, though. Still wearing his hat, he sat there, drinking beer, his booted feet sticking out in front of him. After a long time, he suddenly got up and went over to the corner table where the telephone sat on top of the phone book. He lifted the phone off, set it to one side, and opened the phone book, running his fingers down one of the pages in the middle.

"Yes, sirree, here it is. This'll be the best thing to do now," Cletus mumbled to himself. He closed the book, threw it onto the floor, and slowly began to dial, first a seven, then a three, and the rest of the numbers. By the time he'd dialed the last of the seven digits, he was grinning.

The next night was the dark of the moon and foggy to boot. Heavy white mists lay on the road that led to the Benson place. No one there saw or heard the two figures who crept silently up to the end of the road and went behind the shed where Walt Rose kept Mr. Benson's tractor.

The front door of the house opened just before nine, and out came Cissie's terrier to make his rounds before he took up his sleeping place on the mat in the corner of the kitchen. Letting Spook out and then back inside was the last thing Walt Rose did before he shut off the TV and went up to bed.

Spook made a sniffing tour of the front porch and the yard, then struck out toward the barn and outbuildings closed up for the night.

Suddenly he stopped in the center of the front yard and lifted his head, sniffing. There was something new here, the scent of something interesting. He came padding all at once toward the tractor shed, and he soon found a piece of raw beef on the ground at one corner of the building. The terrier smelled it, then catching it in his teeth, bolted it down. He turned back toward the house, shook his head twice, took a few more steps forward, and fell onto his side.

This was the moment the people behind the tractor shed were waiting for. Swiftly and noiselessly they came out together. The smaller one had a gunnysack with him. He knelt down and held it open while the other bent over, grabbed Spook by his front legs, and shoved him headfirst into the sack. In an instant the dog was inside and hoisted in the sack over the bigger man's shoulder.

Then the pair started away down the private road back to the highway, where they had left a car.

When Walt Rose came out fifteen minutes later to call Spook and then to whistle for him, the two men had completely disappeared into the ground-hugging fog.

Cissie was in bed upstairs. Half in a dream, she heard her father's whistling, and she tossed her head on her pillow. It was a bad dream, one about not being able to find her dog in a dark woods. But the dream passed and merged into one in which she was in Mr. Cameron's class reciting a poem she could only recall half of.

By the time her father came up the steps to bed to tell her mother that "the fool dog must have taken out over the fields after a jackrabbit tonight," Cissie was fast asleep.

Spook awoke the next morning and found himself in an unfamiliar place with queer smells and sounds. He got to his feet and stood wavering dizzily, scenting the air around him. It smelled of tarpaulin, of musty sacks, and of something peppery. Trying to focus his eyes, the terrier stepped forward and was stopped by a wall of rough planking. A couple of steps in any direction took him into more planks, an enclosed pen, something he'd never experienced before. Its wood smelled of gasoline, motor oil, and creosote. Spook prowled his enclosure and saw a bowl of water in one corner. Thirsty, he lapped from it. Then, still groggy, he sank down onto the stained concrete floor beneath him and fell once again into sleep.

When he awoke for the second time, he was not alone. A black-haired, mustached man was staring down at him from the other side of the plank wall. The dog rose to his feet, staring up at the man. Who was he? He smelled him. He was a stranger. The dog's hackles began to rise, and the growl began deep in his throat. When the second man joined the other to rest his forearms on the wall, the growl became a snarling. Spook knew this one. This was the man he'd never liked, the one he'd run at but hadn't reached because a door had been shut between them. All at once the snarl ceased, and Spook launched himself at Cletus Rose, striking the planking with thirty pounds of dog before he fell back onto the concrete.

"Whee! Did you see that?" cried Cletus, taking

off his straw hat and waving it. "Didn't I tell you that this here was some dog, Joe?"

The black-haired man said nothing. However, he smiled and nodded as the dog got to his feet again and, although half-stunned by the first impact, ran at the planks once more.

Finally the dark-haired man said, "I think this one will do. I'll take care of him for you."

"You do that, Joe, and before long this dog'll be taking care of both of us; he's got the makings; he's got the blood in him. He's a natural."

"What is his name?"

"Spook. That's what his folks called him. It means a ghost."

"Ah." The man named Joe stared at the terrier in the pen and said, "Brujo. That's what I'll call him. It means a witch, a man witch."

"I didn't know there was any of them," replied Cletus, "but it don't matter to me. It's a good name, short enough for folks to remember. Now let's get out of this shed and go inside the house where it's cooler. Has your wife got any beer?"

"Yes, Elena will have beer. We'll have one, and then we'll talk about the dog."

Cissie rode off on the school bus crying the next morning. Her dad had told her before breakfast that Spook had gone out the night before but hadn't come back. Because he had never done that before, Cissie began to worry right away. She refused to eat her breakfast except for a piece of doughnut she took with her when she went out hunting for Spook. She whistled and called, "Spook, Spook," in every one of the buildings, but no terrier came running to her. She went out into the fields behind the house, peered into the morning mists, and whistled there, too, but still no dog.

Finally, at the sound of the pickup's horn signaling it was time for her to start for the school bus, she came back to the house.

Her dad was beside the truck with her mother, Darrell, and Lita. "Darrell and I just found something in the barn," he told Cissie.

"Something queer!" Darrell added excitedly.

Cissie cried, "Not Spook! Not my dog! Nothing bad's happened to him, has it?"

"No, not him. Come on, take a look."

Cissie followed her father and the others to the barn, where he pointed to a place under a manger. Cissie peered into the dimness and saw the barn tomcat stretched out on the straw. He wasn't dead. She could tell by the way his chest moved. And there wasn't any blood on his fur to show he was hurt in any way.

Walt Rose said, "The cat's not dead. He's out like a light. I saw him with a little chunk of something just a little while back, less than fifteen minutes ago. I don't know what he was eating or where

70

he got hold of it. I thought maybe it was part of a gopher he caught. But I saw him come around the back of the tractor shed with it in his mouth. He brought it inside here and ate it—and now look at him."

"What in the world?" exclaimed Mrs. Rose.

Lita nodded. "I'll bet that cat's got hold of something that's been doped. It can't be a poisoned rat or gopher he ate, or he'd be dead, too." She turned away from the cat and looked at her aunt. "Aunt Shirley, I bet there was some kind of drug in whatever the cat got hold of."

"Oh, Lita, who would want to drug our barn cats?"

"Maybe it wasn't for the cat, Aunt Shirley."

"Oh, no!" exclaimed Cisse's mother, and she threw a stricken glance at Cissie.

Cissie cried, "You mean somebody came here and doped my dog and took him away?" Her mind raced, and she clutched at her father's arm. "Dad, maybe the cat'll die. If he dies, maybe Spook'll die, too!"

Walt Rose put his arm around Cissie's shoulder. "I don't think so, honey. The cat's breathing okay even if he's out cold. If it'd been poison, the cat would be a goner by this time. And if Spook had got poisoned last night, he most likely wouldn't have traveled any farther than this cat did, and we would have found him. Remember, I looked for him before I even told your mother about his not coming in last night."

Cissie looked up at her father and asked, "Dad, could he have chased a rabbit all the way to the main road and got hit by a car?" She shuddered, remembering Spook's mother.

"I don't think so, Cissie. That's quite a ways from here, and he never went there with you when you caught the school bus. Now you go on to school. I'll keep on calling and looking for him until you get home. I'll watch the cat, too."

Cissie dug her fists into her eyes. "He won't come back, Dad. I know he won't. He's been stolen!"

"Cissie, who'd do a thing like that?" asked Mrs. Rose.

"Uncle Cletus, that's who!"

"You bet that's who, Aunt Shirley," said Lita angrily.

Walt Rose shook his head. "I dunno. But if Spook don't come home by tonight, I'll pay a call on my brother at his repair shop, and if he ain't there, I'll go to his apartment."

"Can I go with you, Dad?" asked Cissie.

"No, Cissie. You better not. I'll go alone."

Sadly Cissie took her lunch box from her mother's hand. With a tearful hug for each of her parents, she started down the road with Lita and Darrell.

By lunch period Cissie was feeling so terrible

that on a sudden whim she went to Mr. Cameron's room. She waited until he was through talking with one of the other teachers and then she told him that the dog she'd written a report about was missing.

"We think somebody put a drug in some meat he got hold of," she said. "Whoever took him must have brought it with him. Do you think that's possible?"

"I don't know," Cameron answered slowly, as he looked at Cissie's troubled face. "This isn't exactly school business, and maybe I shouldn't mix in it," he said, "but there are all kinds of drugs, Cissie. It seems to me, though, that if somebody wanted to knock a dog unconscious he'd have to know a lot about dogs to find a drug that a dog would accept in food."

"I suppose so. Dad says maybe Spook'll be back when I get home tonight."

"Let's hope so. It isn't every day somebody suspects his dog got dognapped. I sure never heard of it before around here, and I've lived in this town all my life."

"I'll tell my mom what you said, Mr. Cameron. She said I should ask you about it."

"Good. I'm glad I could be of some help."

The bell rang just then, and Cissie went out of the room to her first class of the afternoon. Rising from his desk, Mr. Cameron stared after her with a solemn look on his face, then shook his head. He hoped Cissie's trouble would come to a happy ending, and he sighed. Drugging a dog was a queer thing to do.

Spook hadn't returned by the time Cissie and the others got home. Walt Rose reported that his patrol of the main road hadn't turned up anything either. The only good thing he had to report was that the barn cat was all right by now, if a bit groggy. So Spook hadn't been poisoned. Once more Cissie made a search of the Benson property, this time accompanied by Darrell. They found no trace of the terrier anywhere.

That night Cissie lay in bed for hours, thinking about Spook with tears in her eyes. Her father's promise to visit his brother Cletus the next day didn't comfort her much. In her heart she knew now that her dog wouldn't come wandering back home by himself—if he *ever* came back. Only one thing was certain. If Uncle Cletus had Spook, he wouldn't bring him back to her!

Walt Rose drove to the auto-repair shop on La Cadena Boulevard. Weeks before Stella Jane had told Mrs. Rose where her father had set up his latest shop. It was small, dusty, littered, and not doing much business at the moment Walt drove up. That made it like all the other repair shops his brother had run—except for one thing.

Cletus wasn't there!

A gangling young man in grease-stained coveralls came out of the shop. "He ain't here."

"Where'd he go? He's my brother."

"I dunno for sure, Mr. Rose. He said he was goin' away for a couple of days. He said he planned to have himself some fun."

Cissie's father stood beside his pickup truck and asked carefully, "Did Cletus say anything about seeing his girl, Stella Jane?" Had Cletus got wind somehow of where his daughter was and lit out after her?

"I dunno. I never heard him talk about no girl by that name. I didn't even know he had a daughter."

Next Walt Rose asked, "Do you know if Cletus got himself a dog?"

The young mechanic shook his head. "Nope, he never had any dog around here, and I never heard him say he had one where he lives."

"Thanks." Walt Rose got into his truck and drove southward, toward town. Ten minutes later he circled the block on Fourth where he knew his brother lived. The apartment Cletus and Stella Jane had rented was in a two-story stucco building with a single entrance. Somebody else lived on the ground floor. No, Cletus couldn't keep a dog up there, certainly not one that was eager to sink its teeth into him.

Sadly Walt Rose made a left turn and went down Fourth to Magnolia and from there headed for home. Mrs. Rose had promised she'd call the Humane Society and ask if anyone had brought in a gray Staffordshire terrier in the last twenty-four hours. She'd said she had no real hope of Spook's being there, though, and he'd agreed with her. Shirley was a smart woman. That was one of the reasons why Cletus had never taken to her, or she to him. He didn't like smart women.

Walt Rose shook his head as he stopped at a red light at the corner of Magnolia and Van Buren. It would be hard on Cissie to lose her dog, but she'd have to face the fact. He and his family would probably never know where Cletus had gone for "some fun." It was doubtful that he would ever come near them again now that Stella Jane had eloped with Lita's help. Cletus had probably repaid his brother's family for that by stealing Cissie's beloved dog. Now he had better leave well enough alone and not rile old Cletus up even more, or he would for sure do the one thing Walt and his wife feared most. Spook being stolen was bad, but Cletus could do even worse. In time, Cissie would get over the loss of her dog.

*   *   *

Cissie mourned Spook. She sat for hours on the front porch in the swing, staring out over the yard at the tractor shed where the cat had found the drugged meat. She had no appetite and neglected her homework. She refused to have another dog when her dad offered to drive her to the dog pound to pick out a puppy. Mr. Cameron noted her behavior and asked her often if there was any news, but when he saw her eyes brim with tears, he stopped asking.

Two weeks went by, and then one night the phone rang in the Roses' hallway. Auburn-haired Mark, the basketball star, had just driven off in his car with Lita beside him, so the call was probably for somebody else. By now all of the Roses had learned that Lita should answer the phone because just about every call was for her—and from Mark at that.

Cissie answered it on the fourth ring, "Hello."

"Hello. Hello." It was a woman's voice, and she sounded far away. There was a humming sound on the line and a series of clicks and hisses. "Hello, Lita," came the voice again. "This is Stella Jane. I'm calling from Nevada."

"Stella Jane!" cried Cissie. "It's not Lita. It's me, Cissie. Lita isn't here."

"Then please, let me talk to your mother."

"Mom," shouted Cissie. "It's Stella Jane on the phone."

Cissie gave the receiver to her mother, but she stayed nearby, leaning up against the wall next to the instrument.

Cissie heard Stella Jane's reply to her mother's question, "Did you get married?"

"Oh, yes, Aunt Shirley. We got married right away, soon as we could. I'm Mrs. Troy Redpath now. We're sure happy as can be. I wasn't only just scared of my dad but of being out on my own as a wife, but it's working out just fine. Troy's good as can be to me. We're driving from here to where he's got a job waiting in Montana. I'm only calling to say thank you to Lita. She'll know what I mean. Please tell her for me."

"We'll do that. She and Mark went to a movie. We know what she did for you," Mrs. Rose said. "Stella Jane, your dad found that Lita helped you to elope. He came out here. He acted crazy, he was so mad."

"Oh, no!" Cissie heard the telephone wail.

"Yes, he did. Walt told him to get out because Cissie's dog would have attacked him if he hadn't left. Stella Jane, since that happened, we think somebody came here and drugged Spook and took him away. Spook never did come back. Did your father ever talk about anybody who was an expert on dogs or dog medicines? Did Cletus know any vets?"

"No, Aunt Shirley, he sure didn't. Dad and I never even had a dog."

"Stella Jane, did Cletus know anybody in town who did have dogs?"

"No, Aunt Shirley, I don't think he did."

"Think hard, please!"

Cissie held her breath. For a moment there was only a hum on the line and nothing else. Then Stella Jane said, "Somebody once called Dad on the telephone at our apartment. Dad answered the call, so I never heard the voice. But I remember that Dad said something about seeing a couple of dogs someday, and then he said 'Thanks for letting me know' and hung up." Again there was a static-filled pause. Then Stella Jane went on, "That's right. I remember the rest of it now. Dad didn't just say thanks. He said, 'Thanks, Miranda.' "

"Miranda!" exclaimed Mrs. Rose. "A woman?"

"Yes, that's what he said. I'm sure of it."

"Did Cletus have a lady friend in town, Stella Jane?"

For the first time Cissie heard Stella Jane laugh. "Golly, no, Aunt Shirley. I used to pray he'd get one and marry her and have her come keep house for him, so he wouldn't want me around anymore. But he never did. Now I hope he never does. I wouldn't wish that on any woman. Aunt Shirley, this call is plenty expensive. I can't talk any longer.

Give my best to everybody and tell Cissie I'm sorry about her losing Spook, but tell her to keep away from my dad even if she guesses he stole the dog. I think he probably did. It'd be like him if he got mad at all of you the way you say he did. And, please, don't tell Dad where I'm going."

"We won't. Please write us now and then, dear. Thank you for calling, and good luck to you and Troy."

Mrs. Rose hung up the receiver and turned around to face Cissie. "Did you hear it all?" she asked. "You stood so close you were practically in my apron pocket."

"Yes, Mom, I guess I heard everything you did. Miranda. Wasn't that the name she said?"

"Yes, that's what I heard, too. It's strange that Stella Jane should remember a woman's name."

5
Brujo

After he'd walked away from Spook's pen, Cletus
Rose sat drinking beer for over an hour in the tiny
living room of the house on the outskirts of Corona.
Small, dark-eyed Elena Miranda, who'd first shooed
her two little girls off to play in the orange grove
behind the house, did not remain in the room with
the two men once she'd fetched them the bottles of
beer on a tray. She went to the kitchen and seated
herself in the rocking chair in the corner.

Cletus Rose had two swigs of beer out of the bottle. "Okay, then," he said. "Calexico's the next
place, huh? You know somebody there, and you
know it'll be okay for me to come with you?"

Joe Miranda answered, "It will be all right. I can
fix it for you."

"Do you think you can get him in that van of yours without any help?" Cletus asked.

"Yes, I know a way."

"Okay. Say, will you be taking your wife and kids, too?"

Cletus's host chuckled. "No, Elena does not go. She stays home. Come here tonight and leave your car here. We go together in my van. Can you leave your shop?"

"Sure. I'm the boss. Why not? Who needs to know where I go or what I do? Besides I need me some fun, and Calexico sounds like the place for it." Cletus got up, making the springs of the old sofa groan. "All right," he said, "I'll be here at nine. It worked out just fine last night. You sure know a lot about dogs, Miranda."

Joe Miranda told him, "I have worked with dogs before and have been told much about them. I think we got us a good one in Brujo. He ain't much more than a pup, but he's got the blood in him. He will do well, I think."

Later that same day Spook heard footsteps coming toward him and rose up from where he lay. He caught the scent of Joe Miranda and stood without moving, but the man didn't come to look at him. Miranda was busy in a corner, taking some canvas off something. It was a box, and the top and bottom and the two sides were made of solid sheet steel. The two ends were set with steel bars. The man dragged the homemade cage over to the wooden pen and set the barred end next to the planking. A moment later he took down a metal rod that was hanging on the wall and went with it toward the pen.

He stared down at the terrier and nodded. Reaching swiftly over the edge of the pen, the man slid two planks sideways along metal tracks in the floor. The mouth of the cage lay directly in front of the opening.

"Hey, dog," Miranda shouted at Spook, as he reached over the top of the pen with the rod.

Wary of the rod, Spook stepped away from it. The man went swiftly to the side of the pen closest to the dog. He didn't hit Spook with the rod. He only touched him with its point.

The touch of the electric prod used to control cattle made Spook yelp in pained surprise. He lunged at the prod, and Miranda touched the dog again, this time on his left flank, then on his rump. Before Spook could whirl and try to get the prod in his teeth, the man touched the base of the dog's tail.

To escape the sharp shocks, the bewildered Spook went forward, surging toward the section of the pen where the boards had been moved. As the terrier started toward the opening, Miranda touched the bone at the tip of his tail. At that shock, Spook fled out of the pen away from the prod into the cage.

Miranda dropped the prod onto the floor and hurried to the cage to push down the barred end, making Spook a prisoner. Then he slid the boards of the pen back into place.

When Miranda turned around to hang the prod on the wall and go back to the house, he saw that his wife and two little girls were standing together in the wide doorway, watching him.

Elena Miranda explained, "They heard the dog cry out. They came to see, and I came after them."

"Leave this dog alone," Miranda ordered the girls. "Don't go near him. Don't put your fingers in his cage. He does not know you."

"Yes, he belongs to Mr. Rose from another town," said Elena Miranda.

"And half to me, Elena," her husband corrected her. "The dog could make much money for us. You know how I would use that money. It could do much good in my village."

"Yes, I know." The woman sighed. "But I do not like to get money this way. It is against the law of this country, and it is a bad way."

Joe Miranda said nothing as he shut the garage door, leaving a very confused Spook leaning against the side of the cage, his hide stinging.

84

Moments later Spook began to howl and throw himself against the bars and sides of the cage, protesting his imprisonment.

Both Miranda and Cletus Rose were needed to lift the dog's cage into the back of Miranda's closed gray van. All the time they heaved and puffed, Spook yelped, snarled, and threw himself against the sides of the cage. Miranda's scent enraged him as much as Rose's now.

"He's sure full of fight!" exulted Cletus, as he and Miranda shut and locked the back door of the van.

"He will be a good dog," promised Miranda, going around to the front of the van and getting behind the wheel. Once Cletus had joined him, he said, "We've got to cross the desert, and the best way is to go at night when the heat ain't so bad and there ain't so much traffic."

"That's right." Cletus laughed. "We don't want Brujo all tuckered out from heat, do we? We want him fresh as a daisy."

"That's right."

Miranda started the motor of the van Cletus had repaired for him some weeks past. He switched on the headlights. Tomorrow Elena would see to the irrigating of the orange groves belonging to the man who employed him. There wasn't any real heavy

85

work right now, so nobody would miss him if he took a couple of days off.

He could see his wife, silhouetted in the front door with the lights of the living room behind her, and he honked the van's horn in farewell. As Elena waved, the dog behind him in the van began to howl.

"He won't keep that howling up for long," Miranda told Cletus.

"I know that, Joe. He'll get tired of it." Cletus pulled a cigar from his jacket pocket, lit it, and said, "I know a thing or two about dogs myself—even if I don't know how to dope one. What was that stuff you put on those scraps of meat anyhow?"

Miranda didn't reply. He would keep secret the name of the plant he knew about. He only laughed and drove on.

The journey was a long one. Before the van had reached the town of Banning, Spook had stopped howling and throwing his weight against the cage. There wasn't any space for him to prowl back and forth. He stood for a time, bracing himself against the swaying motion of the van. Finally he sank to a crouch and lay there, head on his front paws, looking straight ahead of him at the partition while his ears took in their voices.

Hours later Miranda drove through Calexico to

an isolated house some miles to the east. There he got out, went up to the door, and asked someone something. He was back a minute later, and they drove down a dirt road behind the house into a grove of tall eucalyptus trees sheltering a barn.

The grove was filled with cars, trucks, more vans, and men. Most of the men were younger than Cletus. Some were Mexican-Americans, a few were black, but most were Anglos. Many of them seemed to know Joe Miranda and flocked to his van, surrounding it.

"Hey, Joe, what you got this time?" cried a lanky, blue-eyed man in a checkered shirt.

"I got me a pit bulldog."

"A pit bull? A *real* one?" The man's jaw dropped. "Joe, you got to be kidding. One of them dogs costs over a thousand bucks."

Cletus joined the talk as he got out of the van. "It didn't cost Joe nothing. The dog's half his and half mine. He's a pit bulldog, all right, and he's young. He's got a great future."

Another man, one who was tattooed on the arms with anchors and roses, laughed. "That's what all of you new guys say, mister."

Joe Miranda was out of the van, too, and he introduced Cletus to the men he knew. He used only their first names and the parts of the country they'd come from. Most were from California, Arizona, and Nevada. But there were some men from as far away as Chicago, Miami, North Carolina, Texas, and Alabama.

Finally a very fat man came out of the trees toward Miranda's van. He towered over the others, who made way for him. In a high, husky voice, he told Miranda, "You said your dog's a new one, so that means he's goin' in first."

"That's fine with me, Howie. Howie, this is Cletus. Remember, I called you about him."

"Yeah, okay, get the dog inside. Get the van to the door of the barn, and somebody'll unload that cage you made."

Spook was on his feet the instant Miranda had first got out of the van. He lifted his head to get a scent of where he was and caught the smells of many people, all strangers, except for Miranda and Cletus.

The terrier was standing, facing the van's rear doors when they were opened. He growled loudly, rumbling deep in his chest, when the man called Howie peered in at him. Howie whistled in appreciation. Other men crowded up behind Howie to stare, too, and one muttered, "It sure is a pit bull. A Staffordshire for sure!"

As Miranda and Cletus climbed up into the van to shove the cage forward, Spook went wild with fury. He lunged at the bars at the front end of the cage, trying to break loose.

"Hey, look at that!" cried one of the men.

While Spook flung himself about in the cage, four men hefted it onto their shoulders and carried it to the open door of the barn and inside.

"Okay, let him out. I'm ready for him," Howie told Miranda a moment later. "Everybody keep clear now."

"Okay, Howie."

As the men let go of the cage and stepped back, Joe Miranda came up and swiftly lifted the front bars. Out hurtled the terrier, but he had only three steps of liberty. Howie had been waiting to one side with a strong net, which he threw over the dog. The second after it fell, Howie was onto Spook, rolling him over and over in the net.

"He'll be all right now," said Howie, getting up. "We'll go out and wait for the other new dog. He ain't here yet. He'll be coming in a net, so he won't be no trouble."

The men went out together, leaving Spook in the barn in a shaft of sunlight. As he thrashed in the net, struggling to get loose, he began to howl his anger.

His howl was answered by another howl and then another. There were other dogs in here. Spook sniffed the air. He made out two other dogs, but try as he would he couldn't see them, nor did they come up to him in the net.

A half hour later another dog arrived. He was carried in a net and taken past Spook to a far corner of the building, where he started to howl, too. Soon all four dogs were howling from the four corners of the barn.

Men began to file into the barn, several dozen of them, each paying an admission fee of ten dollars to Howie. Inside they took up positions leaning on top of an enclosure three feet high and fifteen feet square. From there they looked down onto a piece of tarpaulin placed over a carpet on the dirt floor of the barn.

The man from Miami held up a fistfull of bills and yelled, "I got a hundred thirty dollars on the new one called Brujo. On Joe's dog."

"I'll take a hundred of that," called a Chicagoan in a purple T-shirt.

"Two hundred on Brujo," shouted Cletus, and somebody from North Carolina took his bet.

Joe Miranda wasn't at the pen with Cletus. He was with Howie, carrying Spook to the pen, while other men carried the dog that had arrived last of all. Climbing over the sides of the planks, the men took the dogs into opposite sides of the pen, unrolled them from the nets, then grabbed the nets and got hastily over the enclosure to the outside.

Spook found himself facing a black-and-white dog

of mixed breed. It stared at him for only a heart-beat of time. Then silently it leaped toward him, lips pulled back, fangs clashing.

The fighting lust of Spook's ancestors swept through him. For centuries he and his kind had been bred to fight. Now Spook sprang to meet the challenging attack of this strange dog. In a queer, ominous silence the two dogs went for each other.

Spook felt no pain as the stranger fastened his teeth on his left front leg. He jerked free and lunged for the black-and-white animal's throat and tried to catch hold. The stranger pulled back and away, leaving some hide in Spook's jaws. The *scratch, scratch* of the claws of the two dogs were the only sounds to be heard as the audience held its breath. The animals moved about, circling one another, looking for an advantage.

Then the black-and-white, bleeding from the neck, lunged for Spook's front legs again, but the terrier was too swift. Spook whirled away and as the other dog passed him launched himself at the stranger's side. Knocking him off balance, Spook fastened his teeth into his adversary's left ear.

"A ear dog! He's a ear dog!" somebody near Cletus shouted. Then he pounded Cletus on the back, congratulating him.

"Hang on, Brujo," shouted another man.

Spook hung on while the black-and-white thrashed about, rolling over and over with him, kicking him in the belly and sides with his strong legs and sharp claws.

Finally the black-and-white dog, his ear torn half away, managed to pull free. Bleeding heavily from the mangled ear, he leaped up while Spook scrambled to his feet for the next attack. But the stranger turned and ran, heading not toward Spook this time but toward the side of the pit. He tried frantically to leap over its top and fell back onto the tarpaulin.

"It's a turn!" Howie shouted. "Hold the gray one. Hold Brujo!"

"You hold him," bellowed Cletus. "It's your pit."

Cursing in anger, Howie climbed over the wall and expertly caught Spook by the collar, dodging his snapping fangs. He held him with his great strength while the terrier struggled to get at the black-and-white dog. Howie waited for the black-and-white to attack again.

The animal refused. He crouched, shuddering, in a far corner of the pen.

Soon Howie called out, "The gray here's the winner! Get that black-and-white mutt out of here, you guys who own him. Hurry up about it, too. I don't want to hold this dog here all day. Joe, you get the net ready to throw over your dog. He's sure some fighter. He's pullin' my arms out of their sockets."

Five minutes later Spook was out of the net and

back in his cage, still snarling and growling, still eager for a fight.

"Here's your share," Cletus told Joe Miranda, as he gave the other man a wad of money. "Didn't I tell you he was some dog? When is the next fight?"

"Not for a while. It's my turn to have it, and I'll tell you when, but you keep it quiet. Brujo can stay at my place till then unless you got some other place in mind."

Cletus shook his head and said, "Okay, you keep him for us. I can't take him to my place on Fourth Street. I expect my brother's snooping around there and at my shop to see what he can see. It'll come into his head that I took his dog because of what his family did to make me lose my girl. My brother Walt ain't much, but he ain't a fool. His uppity wife always lorded it over me because she thinks *he* got most of the brains in the family. Well, I showed both of them this time!"

In his cage behind the doors of the van, the Staffordshire ceased his noises after a time and started to lick at his leg where it had been mauled by the other dog. He could hear the roaring sounds the men made as they watched the second pair of dogs fighting. Each time they roared, Spook raised his head to snarl. That second match went on far longer than Spook's had, because the dogs were older and more experienced. They were animals famous throughout the West for their courage and blood-thirstiness. Bespattered with blood, they fought for a full half hour until one of them broke and tried to jump the pit as the black-and-white dog had done.

It was past midday before the gathering of cars in Howie's eucalyptus grove broke up, each one heading for a different destination. Several drivers called to Miranda as they passed his van that they were looking forward to watching his Brujo at the next meet.

As they went by, Cletus Rose lifted his hat and nodded to let them know that they'd be there with the gray dog. Soon Miranda joined the line of cars, and Cletus said, "Even if he never saw a pit before, that dog is sure some fighter. My brother showed me a leather dog collar he got off another dog somewheres. I have a hunch that collar is tied up somehow with this dog we got. Most likely it came off another pit bull. The collar had the names Fame and Folly on it. Do they mean anything to you, Joe?"

Miranda shook his head, then suddenly braked his van to a stop next to Howie, who was standing beside the road. "Why don't you ask Howie?" he said to Cletus.

"Okay, I will." Cletus stuck his head past Miranda's and called out, "Hey, Howie, did you ever hear of a dog named Fame or Folly?"

Big Howie scowled at first. Then all at once he nodded. "Yeah," he said, "but it ain't no dog. There's a kennel in L.A. called Fame's. It's plenty fancy, I hear."

Cletus asked, "What kind of dogs do they breed?"

Howie jerked a thumb at the van. "The kind you got in there, pit bulls, Staffordshires, but the dogs they got are show dogs, not fightin' dogs."

An irritated honking from the car in line behind the van made Joe Miranda start up once more.

"Well, well," Cletus said over and over, as they went down the road. "Maybe one of them fancy dogs went astray, huh? It's too danged bad I can't go back and ask my brother some questions about that collar, but it appears to me that I won't be visitin' him no more." He chuckled. "I bet him and his kids, particularly that girl of his, are looking everywhere they can think of for their dog. That'll teach them to try to make a monkey out of me!"

6
"Hurrah for Homework!"

Miranda?

Cissie thought half the night about the name Stella Jane had mentioned. Who could Miranda be? Was it some lady who raised dogs? Ladies were more inclined to raise cats, but they could be dog folks. After all, she was. Who would know about dog folks hereabouts? Who had lived here for a long time?

Mr. Cameron. He was the only person Cissie knew, and he'd most likely know other people who had been here for years too.

Instead of dallying at her locker next morning, Cissie ran to talk to Mr. Cameron the moment she got off the school bus. She still didn't tell him that she believed her Uncle Cletus had taken the dog. She told him only that she had heard that somebody named Miranda might have Spook now.

"Miranda? Miranda? No, I don't know any girl by that name, but I suppose I could ask my fiancée. Kimmie grew up here, too. She and I went to different high schools, so she knows people I don't know. She's got a lot of friends, and she works at the telephone company with dozens of women."

"Oh, please ask her, Mr. Cameron. Ask her for me."

"All right. I'll ask Kimmie tonight when I see her."

Cissie turned away at the sound of the buzzer and took her seat for roll call. Cameron shook his head as he watched her go to her desk. This lost-dog business was getting out of hand. It wasn't his affair, after all.

All that day and evening Cissie looked forward to news of a Miranda, but she got only disappointment when she spoke with her teacher the next morning.

"Okay," he told her. "Kimmie knows two Mirandas. One's a long-distance operator at the phone company, and the other one runs a boutique. She says that they haven't got dogs, either of them. One is allergic to just about everything that has hair, and the other raises tropical fish. Kimmie knows them both pretty well. They can't be the Miranda you're after."

"No, I guess not," Cissie said, holding her civics book tight against her chest. The weight of it somehow helped relieve the weight on her feelings.

"Get yourself another dog," Mr. Cameron advised her. "Go to the pound and get a puppy. Won't anybody take you there?"

Cissie had thought he would be more understanding because he was a teacher. "Dad would take me to the pound, and so would Mark Pringle, Lita's boyfriend, but I don't want to go. I don't want another dog. All I want is Spook. Thank you, Mr. Cameron. Thank your fiancée, too. You tried." Blinking back tears, Cissie went to her seat.

Three more days passed, sad brooding ones for Cissie. She put away her picture of Spook and the report she'd written and tried to forget, but each time one of the barn dogs yelped she ran to the windows to look out, hoping to see her lost terrier.

Cissie had another hard teacher besides Mr. Cameron. He taught geography, and he gave very difficult assignments with lots of homework. On the fourth day after she'd talked to Mr. Cameron about the Miranda lady, the geography teacher gave the class an assignment on agriculture and climate around the world. He wanted a report on a different country from each student. Cissie was assigned Norway. She'd have to hunt up what she could find in the school library about the Norwegian climate and agriculture.

Once again she talked to the school librarian, who gave her a book on Norway that was full of information, which Cissie copied down in her notebook.

When she was finished, the librarian told her, "You might want to make this more up-to-date by looking up the temperature of the capital city for a whole month this year."

"How would I do that for Oslo?" asked Cissie.

"You look in the newspaper put out right here in town. There is a special page devoted to weather. The temperatures and weather conditions of capital cities all over the world are carried there each day."

"Hey, that's sort of neat, isn't it?"

"I think so. The paper's over there on the rack."

"Thanks."

Cissie went to the rack and took the paper down to a table. There she went through the *Press* until she found the weather page. She had never looked at that page before. It was filled with all sorts of information in small print, along with the facts about weather. The small-print things weren't ads. They said who'd been born and who died and who'd got divorced or married. They were called Vital Statistics. The word *vital* made her think. Those things sure were vital, important in people's lives. Cissie didn't bother to read the death and wedding and divorce notices, but she looked at the birth announcements because Mark Pringle's sister had just had a baby boy. She ran her finger down the list, looking for the last name, but it wasn't there yet. Her eyes followed the births to the very last line and stopped all at once, riveted by the final tiny item. She sat staring at it until the buzzer to change classes rang, and then she left the library almost at a run for Mr. Cameron's room with her finding. Even if he didn't seem all interested and had suggested she replace Spook, she was going to tell him.

Standing at his desk, she gasped out, "I saw where a Mr. and Mrs. Miranda had a baby girl in Indio last week. Oh, Mr. Cameron, can Miranda be a man's last name?"

"Why, yes, it could, but I don't know anybody myself by that name." His forehead was wrinkled in deep thought, and he sighed as he said, "You know, this problem of yours is weighing on my mind. I've thought of something else since we talked last time. Why don't you call veterinarians and ask if they know anybody named Miranda who keeps dogs? That's probably what you should have done in the first place. Thinking you had only a girl's name threw everybody off. How'd you come to think of Miranda as a last name?"

Cissie told him of Norway and of the geography

100

assignment and the newspaper and the vital statistics. Mr. Cameron chuckled and said, "Well, hurrah for homework! See what you can get out of homework sometimes?"

"Yes." Cissie nodded. "That's how I learned my dog was a pit bulldog."

"Well, Cissie, it seems to me the next thing you ought to do is look in the yellow pages of your phone book for veterinarians and call them up and ask if any one of them knows somebody by the name of Miranda who has dogs." Cameron leaned back in his chair. "It'll be a lot of work for you, and probably you'll have to hang on the phone for a while, but it's the best thing you've got going for you so far."

"I guess so. I'll do it for sure Saturday." Cissie hesitated, then said, "Mr. Cameron, thank you for the help you're giving me. We've got lots of troubles in my family. I can't talk about 'em, though. My folks and I have had trouble over and over in lots of places. That's why we've moved around so much."

Cameron nodded understandingly. "Let's hope you won't have to move again," he said. "I'd say this town seems to agree with you. I remember your cousin well. How's Lita doing these days? She was a good student."

"She's doing all right," Cissie said. And thanking Mr. Cameron again, she turned away, heading for the corridor and her locker.

She didn't want to talk anymore. As she leaned against the cool metal of the locker she was wishing she could tell her teacher how she suspected Uncle Cletus, how shady and crooked he was in his dealings, and how Lita figured he had something on her dad. What Lita had hinted at stuck like a bone in Cissie's throat, but she knew she dared not ask her father or mother about it. Asking would make trouble for her and for Lita, too, and what if Lita had been wrong all along? That would surely hurt her dad's feelings when he'd worked so hard paying off bills Uncle Cletus had run up in other states. Mom had worked hard, too, being a waitress in Washington State while Dad had been away those years in the Army. They had been extra hard years for her and Darrell and Lita, because they'd all been so poor. What little Mom had left over from her paycheck and tips after home expenses was used to pay off those business bills Dad and Cletus had owed.

Well, this was Rose family business, and they seemed to be rid of Uncle Cletus at last. What was really bothering her now was finding Spook. Saturday was coming up, only two days away. Maybe it would be a lucky day for her. She sure hoped so.

The horoscope in the paper was promising. It said that Librans should make progress if they exerted themselves.

First Cissie made a list of the vets in the yellow pages; then she got Lita to promise not to complain if she tied up the phone line for a couple of hours when Mark might be trying to call.

"Sure," said Lita, who'd just tinted her hair an even lighter shade of blond. She was standing in front of the hallway mirror, lifting it up and letting it fall, trying to decide if she wanted to cut and curl it.

Cissie started down her list of veterinarians, always asking the same questions of whoever answered the phone. "Do you know anybody named Miranda who raises dogs?"

Generally a lady answered, and she would say, "You mean kennel people, of course. Miranda *who*, please? What's the last name?"

Cissie would say, not betraying that it wasn't only kennel people she was after, "It might not be a first name. Maybe it's a lady's last name or her first name or a man's last name. I don't know which, but it's somebody who has dogs."

Then the person at the vet's office would say, "Oh, just a minute. I'll go look in the card file for any Miranda we might have who has dogs for sale."

Cissie would wait, chewing at a hangnail, until the person came back. What they said was always the same, even if the words were different. "I'm sorry, but no one by that name has ever brought any animals here."

Cissie would say thank you and go on to dial the next number.

There were thirty-six vets and animal hospitals in the several towns near Mira Loma. Seven of them didn't doctor anything but large animals, mostly horses. Another listing in the phone book puzzled her. A trip to the dictionary told her that "Practice Limited to Equine" also meant horses only.

In all she had to make twenty-four phone calls to doctors who treated small animals. In three hours of waiting for twenty-four ladies to look through their files, she came up twenty-four times with, "Sorry, we haven't got any Mirandas."

As she hung up the phone for the last time, there were tears in her eyes. "Okay, Lita, the phone's free now," she called out in spite of her unhappiness. "I didn't have any luck at all," she added.

Lita, who'd grown nicer and kinder ever since Spook had been stolen, appeared at once from the living room. Sadly Cissie asked, "Oh, what'll I do now?"

"I'm fresh out of ideas myself, Cissie, but why don't you ask Mr. Cameron if he's got any other suggestions?"

Turning away, Cissie rubbed at her eyes. "Maybe he's going to get tired of me pestering him so much. I wouldn't blame him if he did. He says it isn't school business, and he's right."

"I'm sure sorry," said Lita, stroking Cissie's hair and looking at her mournfully.

In spite of her misgivings, Cissie did go to Mr. Cameron two days later to report on the twenty-four phone calls she'd made. She had decided she owed him the report because he was the one who had suggested it to her.

He balanced a rubber eraser on his palm for a moment, then said, "This gets deeper, doesn't it? Use your head, Cissie. There are other towns hereabouts, and they have vets in them, too."

"Should I try to get in touch with them about a Miranda, too?

"Well, it's your dog you're after, isn't it?"

"But if I called them, it'd be long distance." Cissie thought of Stella Jane's complaint that her long-distance call was expensive. "I'd have to wait till the ladies looked in their card files for me, and that takes up more time and would cost Dad more money."

"Well then, don't call them. Write them. Go to the public library and look in the out-of-town phone books, in the yellow pages. Copy down the addresses of the vets and write to them. Put a stamped postcard with your address written on the front of it inside your letter so they'll answer you if they have a Miranda on their books."

Cissie stared open-mouthed at Mr. Cameron. She would never have thought of that.

He went on, "Try San Bernardino, Palm Springs, Redlands, and Corona." He shook his head. "It'll take time and money, but it just might turn up a Miranda somewhere."

"All right, I'll go to the public library next Saturday morning, write letters the rest of the weekend, and mail them on Monday."

That Monday morning Cissie, using all the allowance money she had, put fifty letters into the mailbox on the road. The very same morning Joe Miranda entertained a very important guest.

Leon (the Deacon) Gates arrived, driving a shining gold-color sedan that made Joe's eyes grow wide. As the tall black man slipped out of the driver's seat Joe's eyes grew even wider. Even the Deacon had never looked so elegant. His suit was a pale fawn color, and he wore beige shoes and a maroon shirt open at the neck to show gold chains at his throat.

The two little Miranda girls went behind their father to stare shyly at the newcomer. "Go to your mother. Don't bother us," Joe ordered them, and they fled at once.

At her husband's swift gesture toward her, Mrs. Miranda turned about and hurried to the rear of the house. Joe knew that she was wary of Gates. She had told him once that the air of coldness and power that flowed from Gates scared her. Joe understood what she meant, but he admired the Deacon more than he feared him.

Joe Miranda greeted his guest warmly. The Deacon only nodded at him in return. Then he said in a deep, musical, cool voice, "Where's this dog you called me about, Miranda? Let's get on with it."

"He's in there, in a pen," Miranda told his guest. "We can't let him loose."

"Okay, show me. You said he did real good in Calexico, and he's an ear dog, huh?"

"That's right. He's a young dog, too. I don't own him alone, Deacon. I look after him, but he's only half mine."

Gates said nothing as he went with Miranda to the garage, where strings of red peppers hung drying on the sunniest wall.

Spook had heard the tires of Gates's car crunching on the gravel in front of the house, and he got up in the pen.

Thanks to the electric prod, the weeks spent with Joe Miranda had changed him. He no longer howled or barked in his enclosure, though each time Miranda came near him, he snarled. He had learned to permit the man to prod him out of the pen and tie him onto a homemade treadmill for exercising. While he walked on the treadmill, Elena cleaned his pen and put down fresh water and food.

Spook scented the newcomer, Gates, getting the odor of cologne and of cigars. This stranger was the first one he'd seen in quite a while. The terrier's lips lifted to bare his teeth.

Gates didn't lean on the top of the pen the way Joe Miranda and Cletus Rose did each Saturday afternoon while they discussed the upcoming fight meets. Gates gazed down at the dog and murmured after a bit, "I like the looks of this one, Miranda. Better than I liked the last one, that half collie, half shepherd you had."

"You were right, Deacon. He wasn't half as good a dog as this one. This is a Staffordshire, a real pit bull like I told you over the phone."

"What happened to your other dog?"

"He got chewed up by a dog from Fresno. He was so bad that the vet my wife took him to couldn't save him. She went to that guy in Corona you told me about."

"Too bad. Okay, I'll get to watch this one pretty soon, huh?"

"You won't be sorry you came to see him, Deacon. I'll call you when it's time. Right now I don't have the date set up for sure."

"You do that, Miranda, and before you call me talk to your partner. Take good care of the dog in there." The Deacon gestured with a long hand that flashed with rings.

Joe escorted Gates back to the gold-colored car. "The Staffordshire dogs are worth much money," he said.

Gates asked, "Does your partner know that?"

"Yes. A man in Calexico was telling us both about them."

The Deacon looked at Miranda, nodded his head, and opened the door of his fancy car. A moment later he was backing skillfully out onto the narrow road that led to the Miranda house.

Joe stood for a while staring after him, then went up to the house, smiling. Once inside he went to the telephone and began to dial number after number from a list he took out of his pants pocket.

Two days after she'd sent out the letters, Cissie began to look for replies. Lita told her, "Give it a little time. The vets have barely got the letters. It'll take a while for their office girls to look in their files."

"Hey, do the vets keep their files under the names of dogs or cats instead of people?" Darrell asked.

Cissie laughed, her first laugh in a long time. "Oh, Darrell, the vet can't send his bill to a dog. He has to send it to the person who owns a dog."

Lita tapped Cissie on the shoulder. "Wow! You're getting smarter all the time, Cissie Rose!"

A week passed without a single postcard showing up in the mailbox. But the following Monday afternoon, when she came home from school, Cissie found a card of hers among some mail for her parents.

The card was from Dr. Sharpe, and it came from Corona. Neatly typed, it was brief. All it said was that he had a Miranda, an Elena Miranda, in his files, but it was against his policy to give out the addresses of his patients' owners.

"Corona?" exclaimed Cissie. "A *lady* in Corona!"

"Let me see." Lita took the card, read it, and said, "Hmm, it doesn't say this Elena Miranda even has dogs, does it? Maybe she's got rabbits or hamsters?"

"Or snakes or turtles. What'll you do now, Cissie?" asked Darrell

Cissie had a quick answer. "I'll take the card to Mr. Cameron and ask him, but first I'm going to call Information and see if there is a Elena Miranda in Corona."

Cissie spoke to her teacher the next morning before she even went to her locker to put her jacket away. She handed him the postcard and said, "This came yesterday. I called up Information and asked for a Elena Miranda in Corona, but they don't have anybody by that name who has a phone. They've got some other Mirandas, but they aren't named Elena."

Mr. Cameron rubbed his chin for a moment, then said, "Maybe she's married to one of those Mirandas, Cissie."

"Maybe so. What do I do now?"

"Well, it seems to me that what you might do is go to see this vet and ask him some questions. Can you get transportation there?"

"I think so. Dad's mostly busy on Saturday mornings. That's when he drives into Riverside to do some shopping. But Mark Pringle could take Lita and me. I think he's supposed to come over then."

"Good enough."

All at once a thought struck Cissie. "Hey, shouldn't we have an excuse to go see Dr. Sharpe? Maybe we should have a sick animal?"

Mr. Cameron gave Cissie a smile. "Good thinking. Have you got a sick animal?"

"There's our old tomcat. He looks pretty sick most of the time."

"Take him then."

"We can say he's got a cold or fever or something." Cissie managed a grin. "All we have to do is catch him. Oh, Mr. Cameron, do you think it'll work? Do you think we'll find out about Elena Miranda from the vet?"

"I don't know, but you deserve some luck. You've

111

worked hard making all those phone calls and writing all those notes. Still, hard work doesn't always mean success in things, Cissie."

Cissie nodded sadly. "I guess not. But I sure did work. And I used up all my money." She brightened. "But Mom'll give me some so we can pay the Corona vet for just the one time. Mom sure liked Spook, too."

When Mark Pringle called Lita that night, Lita gave him Cissie's request, and he agreed to drive them to Corona to see Dr. Sharpe.

Cissie heard Lita say into the telephone, "Cissie's dad can't do it for her, but her mom'll give us the money for the vet. Hey, Mark, have you got a wicker basket we can put our cat in? The cat's our alibi to see the vet." There was a pause in the conversation. Then Lita said, "Well, we haven't got a basket either. All we've got are boxes, and the cat'll get out of those, he's so strong." Lita giggled as she listened and said, "Oh, sure we've got towels. Cissie can sit in the back seat and hold him. Okay, see you at ten o'clock, Mark." Again Lita listened. Then she cooed, "Sure. Sure I do, Mark. You know I do."

"Oh, mush!" said Cissie, as she turned away to go tell her mother they'd be driving to Corona with Mark on Saturday.

What a chase Cissie and Darrell had and what a

battle the cat put up the next morning! The old tom led them through every building on the place until he'd been cornered at the top of the pepper tree and grabbed by the two children, who climbed the tree after him. While Lita and Mark called up advice from below, Darrell caught the spitting cat by his hind legs while Cissie threw a pink bath towel over him. Then, holding the cat, she climbed down to the ground. He scratched her all the way.

After she and Darrell were down, Darrell said, "I'm glad I'm not going with you this morning. I don't want any more of that wild cat."

"Thanks for helping, Darrell," Cissie told her brother.

The drive down lovely Victoria Avenue, all roses and palm trees, would have been pleasant if Cissie hadn't had the cat to struggle with. She was glad when they were finally on the outskirts of Corona and traveling down a heavily congested street. They ought to be pretty close to Dr. Sharpe's now. Cissie had no time to watch for street signs because the cat twisted about so much, so Lita took on the chore.

After a time Lita pointed to a building on their right and cried, "That's it, Mark. Over there. The low stucco buildng, the brown one."

"I see it," he said. "The one that says *Small Animal Hospital*." Mark pulled his little yellow car into the parking lot and turned off the ignition.

The Staffordshire Terror

Lita said, "We'll all go in together. We'll gang up on that vet. Cissie, is the cat wearing you out?"

"He sure is."

"Okay then, Mark can take him in."

"All right. Be careful, though. He sure wants out in the worst way." Cissie waited until Mark and Lita got out. Then she gave the cat to him with the words, "Don't let go of him for a second, or we'll lose our alibi to see the vet."

"I got him," said Mark, as he took the cat. He spoke to the snarling animal, "Hey, look sick, cat."

The three of them sat for a time in the doctor's waiting room while Mark held the cat. He struggled even more here because of the other animals mewing and barking in baskets and in their owner's arms. Cissie gave her name and the name of the cat —Thomas Rose—to the office lady.

Finally they were called to the examining room where they met Dr. Sharpe, a chunky man in a long, green cotton coat.

"What seems to be the trouble with this animal?" he asked. "He seems lively enough to me." By this time the cat was out of the towel and on the table. Both Dr. Sharpe and Mark were needed to hold him down.

Cissie answered, "He acts sort of strange at times. Mom says he's off his feed lately, too."

"Well, we'll get his temperature and see. Do all three of you own him?"

114

"No, mostly me, I guess. It took all of us to get him here, though." Cissie looked around the room, noticing the glass cases of instruments. She decided the time had come to start trying to get information. "A lady I know says you're a real good vet. She said for us to come here with our sick animals."

"Well, that's nice to hear. Who's the lady?" Dr. Sharpe asked, after he'd started taking the cat's temperature.

"Elena Miranda. She's a friend of my mom's." Cissie held her breath. "She said you were really good when it comes to sick dogs."

Dr. Sharpe grunted. "I'm happy to hear she feels that way after what happened with that dog she brought to me. She was crying when she brought him in, wrapped up in an old blanket. I only wish I could have saved him for her, but he was dying even then. He was a fine animal, half collie, half German shepherd."

Cissie's heart began to beat again. It wasn't Spook! She said, "Mrs. Miranda never told Mom about that, I guess. Was her dog hit by a car?"

"No. He'd been mauled, bitten in a number of places, and he had bad internal injuries besides. All those bites weren't caused by a car. When I asked Mrs. Miranda what the dog had been fighting, she told me it was a pack of wild dogs." The vet shook his head. "Those dogs that run wild sure make a lot of grief for everybody. She told me that her hus-

115

The Staffordshire Terror

band had a hard time beating off the wild dogs."

Fishing for information, Lita cleverly asked, "Isn't her husband the Frank Miranda who has a shoe store here?"

"I don't know what he does hereabouts, but as I recall she called him Joe. I never met him myself."

Dr. Sharpe took the thermometer from Thomas Rose and said, "He's got a little bit of temperature, but that could be due to his being upset. Let me examine him now." As the vet ran his hands over the wild-eyed cat, then looked into his mouth and ears, Cissie asked, "Do the Mirandas raise dogs?"

"Not that I know about. Mrs. Miranda only came to me the one time. She said she didn't know where to go with the dog at first, but a friend of her husband gave her my name as a nearby veterinarian. I didn't know him, but he had such an odd name it stuck in my mind. It was Deacon Gates. I guess he must be some official in the church the Mirandas go to."

"*Deacon?*" echoed Lita.

"That's right. Well now, your cat appears to be all right to me. Don't worry about him. I'll give you some vitamins for him. Watch and see how he eats from now on, and if he gets listless or his fur gets spiky and his eyes seem glazed over, bring him back to me."

To Mark, Dr. Sharpe said, "You can take care of the bill at the desk."

116

To Cissie, he said, "When you see Mrs. Miranda again, I don't think you ought to mention their dog dying. She was pretty upset over it, and I wouldn't remind her if I were you."

"We sure won't. I'll tell Mom not to, too. Thanks, Dr. Sharpe," Cissie said, while Mark got Thomas Rose back into his pink towel once more.

Once they'd paid the bill and were back inside Mark's car and on the way home, Lita said, "Boy, we sure found out plenty, didn't we?" She turned to look triumphantly over her shoulder at Cissie, who sat in the back seat with the towel-wrapped cat in her lap and his vitamin drops in her jacket pocket.

Over his yowling, Cissie answered, "I guess so, Lita, but we still don't have Spook."

7
The Next Meet

Mark dropped Cissie and Lita at their house and drove off to do some errands for his mother.

"Well, what did you find out?" Shirley Rose asked the girls, as they came inside.

Cissie replied, "We found out that a Mrs. Miranda took a dog once to Dr. Sharpe, the vet in Corona. Her half collie was hurt, and he died. The vet thought maybe she called her husband by the name of Joe. I think there's a Joe Miranda who has a phone in Corona."

"What will you do if there is? Have you thought about that?"

"I'll call up his house and ask anybody who answers the phone if there's a gray Staffordshire terrier there."

Mrs. Rose shook her head as she switched off her

steam iron. "Wait a minute. Don't do that. If this Miranda helped your Uncle Cletus get hold of Spook, he certainly isn't going to tell you that he's got your stolen dog, Cissie."

"I guess not." Cissie sat down heavily next to the ironing board. "What should I do now, Mom? Call the police?"

Mrs. Rose looked down at the blue chambray workshirt she was ironing for her husband. She said slowly, "I think the best thing would be to go there with me tomorrow. See if you can find out where this Miranda lives. If Spook's there and he hears your voice or gets your scent, he'll make such a racket barking you won't have to ask about your dog. Then we can have the police get your dog back."

Lita asked, "What about mean old Cletus?"

"Don't mention his name to anybody. Keep Cletus out of things if you possibly can."

"What if he's there when we go, Aunt Shirley?"

"I doubt that he will be. His shop and apartment are in Riverside, quite a distance from Corona, and besides you don't know for sure that these Mirandas, whoever they are, have anything to do with Cletus or your dog. You may be barking up the wrong tree entirely. We'll go tomorrow. I'll take you in the pickup."

Five minutes later Cissie and Lita sat in the porch

swing with glasses of lemonade in their hands. Cissie
was long faced and so was Lita until all at once Lita
snapped her fingers. "I got it, Cissie. Why wait till
tomorrow to hunt up Miranda? Mark's coming here
again tonight. He and I are supposed to go to a
movie out at the Mall, but instead we'll go back to
Corona and have a look around all on our own. He's
plenty interested in Spook, too. It'll be an adventure. You can come too."

"Oh, Lita, you're such a lot of help to me. Thank
you. Would Mark mind?"

"No, of course not. I'll fix it and tell your mom
and dad that I'm treating you to a movie to take
your mind off your dog for a while."

"Would you, Lita?"

"Yes. Go call Information and get the address of
any Joe Miranda you can find. Don't worry about
our not being able to find the address. Mark's got
stacks of road maps and town maps. He can find
any place."

Cissie got up at once. She went to the phone,
dialed 411, and asked for the telephone number of a
Joe Miranda in Corona. The operator gave it to
her and then, when she asked, gave her the address,
too. It was much like Cissie's own, a number on a
rural route, but the country road also had the name
of Dailey.

Cissie ran back to Lita, flung her arms around her

neck, and whispered, although she felt like shouting, "I got it! A Joe Miranda lives on Dailey Road."

"Fine. Okay." Lita disengaged herself, laughing. Then she shook a finger at Cissie. "Now don't get your hopes up too much. Remember, you could be barking up the wrong tree like your mother says. Your astrology for today said to be careful and expect the worst."

"Oh, Lita, all I want to hear is Spook barking—anywhere. My astrology most always says bad things."

Cletus Rose steamed into the space before Miranda's house a couple of minutes after five o'clock, parked his car, and lumbered to the garage where his partner kept the dog. As he went inside, he noticed that the back doors of the van parked just outside were open.

"Hey, Joe, I'm here. It's me, Rose." Cletus came into the building and, as he did, was greeted with the sudden barking of the Staffordshire, followed by yelps and snarling sounds.

Cletus chuckled. The dog sure hadn't forgotten who he was.

"Come on," Joe Miranda called. "I'm gettin' ready to put him in the cage. You can help me load him in the van. I just put wheels on the cage to make it easier to push it up the ramp."

The Staffordshire Terror

Cletus sauntered to the pen to lean on it, watching Miranda, who had the electric prod in his hand again.

Miranda didn't have to touch the dog with it; he only pointed it at him. By now Spook knew its power all too well. He let himself be maneuvered by it to the side of the pen and into the cage as Miranda gestured, first at one part of the dog's body, then at another.

"Pretty good," Cletus remarked admiringly. Then he asked, "I thought you was to hold the meet tonight, Joe? How come you're putting the dog in the van?"

Miranda raised his voice to be heard over Spook's yelping in the cage. "We go to the place I know near Colton. It's where I go when it's my turn. This garage is too small, and then there's my family, too." Miranda hung up the prod.

"I see," Cletus said. "Will fat Howie be there?"

Miranda came nearer so Cletus could hear him better. "I think he will. He likes to be a referee. The Deacon is coming, too. I called him, and I told him where we are to go. He wants to see Brujo fight tonight."

Cissie's uncle nodded. "Yep," he said.

The two men got Spook's cage rolled up the board ramp set beneath the rear of the van. Then Miranda shut the van's doors, got behind the wheel, and drove off.

122

After he'd gone, his wife came out and stared after the van. One of her small daughters ran over to the car Cletus had parked and began to climb up onto its hood.

"Don't do that!" scolded Mrs. Miranda. "Leave that car alone. Come into the house."

It was six when Mark, Cissie, and Lita pulled up at the mailbox with the name Joe Miranda painted on it. The signpost on the road beside it was dusty but readable as Dailey Road.

"Okay, here we go," Mark told the girls, as he swung his small car onto Dailey Road. He had been delighted at the prospect of an adventure.

Cissie crossed her fingers and kept them crossed while they jolted down this road, which was bumpier and narrower than the old Benson Road. Would she find the right Miranda here? Would she find Spook? What would these people who lived here say to Mark? Reluctantly she and Lita had come to the conclusion that Mark ought to ask the questions. Mark might get more information alone without them because he looked so grown-up and had such a deep voice for seventeen. Besides even if Cissie sat in the car, Spook could get her scent with his wonderful nose. She planned to whistle for him from the car. She certainly would look silly if she whistled on the porch all the time Mark was talking to whoever lived in the house.

Cissie let out a sigh. She hated lying to her folks about the movie, but it had been only a half lie at that. If Spook wasn't here and they'd come to the wrong place, they could still make the movie.

Dailey Road dead-ended in an orange grove. There were only two buildings there, a garage with its doors closed and a little white house.

And something else!

Sitting in the back seat, Cissie grabbed suddenly at Lita's shoulder in front of her and pointed. "Look! Look at the cream-colored car! I think it's the one Uncle Cletus had when he came to our house that last time."

Lita cried out softly, "Hey, I think it is, too! I remember the license plate. It has my initials— LMH. It's the right color, too."

"Turn around, Mark," Cissie begged. "I don't want to run into Uncle Cletus."

"Don't do it, Mark. Scrooch down, Cissie!" As Lita sank down onto the front seat her voice floated over to Cissie, who'd at once slid down out of sight, too. "Cletus never set eyes on Mark. He won't know why Mark's coming here. You and me, Cissie, we'll keep hidden, and Mark can still go up to the door."

"Sure," Mark agreed. "I'll ask where's the nearest gas station."

"Wait first, please. Don't go up just yet. Let me do something first." Cissie leaned her head out of the car window on the side opposite her uncle's parked car and whistled softly. She waited. Spook knew that whistle well!

There was no barking in return, no terrier running through the trees to her.

"Okay, the dog isn't here," said Lita nervously. "Okay, Mark."

Mark stopped the engine and got out, heading for the front door of the house.

Before he rapped on it, he looked through its glass into the tiny living room. There was no one inside but a small, dark-haired woman embroidering and two little girls looking at the pictures in a magazine. He could see straight throughout the house into the kitchen in back. There was no one at the kitchen table either.

Mark knocked. Neither Joe Miranda nor Cletus Rose seemed to be there. This woman, who looked up so very startled at his knock, might be Elena Miranda all the same, the Elena Miranda who'd brought the dog to the vet in Corona.

"Who is there?" she cried out, getting up from her chair. Her voice sounded plenty scared.

Mark caught her fright and called back. "I'm in a hurry, lady. I don't want to come in." He changed his mind about asking for a gas station and decided to come to the point fast. "I came here about a dog," he said instead.

She called to him, "My husband is gone. If you came here about a dog, you must know where he is." She came up to the door to stare at Mark through the glass at its top, but she didn't open the door to him.

"I forgot how to get there," he told her. Then another idea struck him. "Hey, isn't that Mr. Rose's car by the house? I know him."

"Yes, it is. He went with my husband in the van —and with Brujo, too. They all went to Colton, the place they always go to."

"Colton? Oh, sure, but I forgot how to get there. Your husband never gave me a map."

"It is the barn, the old one that no one uses anymore. It is not far from the *asistencia*, the outpost that the priests built a long time ago as part of the old mission."

"Sure, the old adobe? I know that. I can find the barn okay. Thanks." Inspired by a hunch, Mark asked, "How's Brujo doing? I guess he's Joe's new dog, huh?"

He saw the woman's pretty face darken. "Like something wild, this one is. A wild animal, not a dog at all."

"Thanks again." Mark spun on his heel and left, running to his car. As he got in, he told the concealed girls. "Get up! It worked. Joe Miranda and your Uncle Cletus, Cissie, went to Colton, and they took a dog named Brujo with them. I know where they went—to an old barn."

Lita, who bumped her head on the dashboard getting up, asked, "How did you find out all that, Mark?"

"I only mentioned the word *dog* to Mrs. Miranda, and she told me everything I needed to know. I think she got the idea that I was somebody her husband knew real well."

Cissie asked, "Brujo? Did you say the dog was named Brujo?" She felt sick with disappointment.

"That's the name she used."

Lita said to Cissie, "Wait. Don't give up now! It could be Spook. Somebody could have changed his name, but it could still be Spook!"

Mark added, "Mrs. Miranda said he was like a wild animal, not a dog at all. All right, hang on, you two. We won't be going to the movies tonight. Colton, here we come! I want to see some men about a dog!"

Cissie, who'd slumped down in the rear seat said, "Okay, be funny, if you want to, but what are this Miranda and my Uncle Cletus doing with my dog?"

"That's what we're going to find out," Lita vowed fiercely. "Whatever it is, I bet it's not good," she added under her breath.

It took Mark thirty minutes to reach their destination, a cluster of old buildings, some large, some small, that had once been a horse ranch. Now all were abandoned and decaying. Mark knew that the old gray barn, the largest building, lay behind the others because as a little boy he'd played in it with his cousins, who once lived nearby. It had an unusual feature of an outside stairway, which was something used on old Spanish- and Mexican-style buildings but rarely on barns. He even knew why the stairway was there. In the old days the ranch hands had slept in a room adjacent to the hayloft. He and his two cousins had explored it once and then left hastily because of its spookiness. It had been only a shell, one wall in front of the loft and a wall separating it from the hay.

Mark didn't drive into the old ranch. Most likely Joe Miranda and Cletus Rose were there, and he thought they should be very careful now. Instead he parked his car under pepper trees on the road a distance from the barn and told the girls, "Come on. We'll walk over the fields so nobody'll spot us. There used to be stairs at the back of the barn. We'll go up them and inside the loft. If we keep quiet, nobody even ought to know we're there."

"Mark," said Lita, "I'm scared!"

He stopped. "Look, you roped me in on this. I'm getting more and more curious about it. If those two guys have Cissie's dog, don't you want to know about it?"

128

Standing apart from the other two, Cissie said very softly, "Yes, I want to know."

"Come on then." Mark pulled apart some ancient rusted strands of barbed wire and pointed wordlessly to the little building next to the barn. There was a van parked beside it.

Mark peered at it through the twilight, then muttered to the girls, "There's nobody sitting in it. That means they're inside and won't be seeing us out here in the field. Come on. Follow your leader, girls."

The three of them veered to the left and passed under more barbed wire. Silently they approached the rear of the barn. There Mark halted and pointed upward to the flight of wooden steps with a sagging railing alongside. He went up first, testing each step for soundness with his large foot before stepping on it. The girls came after him, first Cissie, then Lita. The steps made some creaking noises, but they were covered by the grating sounds of the ranch's old windmill a short distance away. The door at the top was half open. Mark slipped through it, and the girls followed.

Standing just inside, Cissie held her breath until her eyes grew used to the semidark of the musty old loft.

Lita whispered, "What'll we do now?"

Mark hissed back, "Lie down on the floor. They've got lights on. They're down there. The floor's full of cracks. Find a knothole if you can."

Cissie lay down, feeling the blown-in dirt and dust of years crunching under her while she looked for the light that meant a crack or knothole in the boards under her.

Mark was right. There was light below, a yellow glow. As she gazed, it got brighter and brighter. Someone down there was lighting kerosene lanterns, one by one. Then she saw a dark-haired man cross her field of vision with a lantern in each hand. Joe Miranda? More than likely it was.

She heard him call out, "The boards are stacked in the corner from the last time, and the tarpaulin and carpet's rolled up there, too. How about taking the canvas off them?"

"Okay, Joe." That was her Uncle Cletus's voice for sure.

Cissie felt Lita's hand touch hers to let her know she'd recognized it, too.

Where was Spook? Where was her dog? Cissie gnawed at her knuckle while she watched her uncle and Miranda put down a carpet on the old boards of the barn floor and cover it with a tarpaulin. The tarpaulin was ringed about by lanterns. What on earth were they up to? As she watched they left together for another part of the barn and returned.

They were carrying things that looked like big wooden doors, but they had hinges on each end, not just on one side. When they had a whole stack of them piled onto the floor, the men set to work fitting

130

the panels together, end to end, hinge to hinge, until they'd erected a good-sized square.

"All right, that's done it," Cissie heard Miranda say. "Now let's go out and wait for them to come." The two men walked out of her line of sight.

Cissie whispered to Lita and Mark, "I don't see any dog."

Mark answered her question. "It's most likely in the van."

"Spook? In the van we saw?"

"Yes." Lita's hand was on Cissie's left arm. "And don't you think of going down there to see! Remember what the men said just now. There are others coming here."

Mark added, "Yes, they could be all over the place, Cissie. I'm going to the door and look at the road."

Cissie heard him scrambling past her feet and saw his large, dark silhouette in the doorway. He stayed there for a while, then came softly back to lie down again. "More cars are coming. There are a lot of headlights out on the road I parked on. Something's going to happen here all right." He didn't add what he thought it was. Instead he said in his deepest rumble, "Cissie, remember, whatever it is that's going to happen down there, you be quiet! We don't want anybody to find out that we're up here. If you spot your dog, don't whistle or call his name or do anything at all."

"Why not, Mark?"

The Staffordshire Terror

"Because if your uncle and this Miranda have gone to all this trouble to arrange something way out here, it will be against the law. Getting caught while you watch people do things against the law can be dangerous. Cissie, has your uncle ever done anything illegal?"

Before the trembling Cissie could reply, Lita said, "You bet he has!"

Mark said, "Well, there's your answer, Cissie. Cissie, how are you doin'?"

With an effort Cissie kept her voice from breaking. "Okay. I'm okay. Uncle Cletus won't find out that I'm up here."

She lay on the hard floor watching the pen below while she listened to the sounds of car doors shutting, men's talking and easy laughter, and now and then the baying yelp or bark of a dog. There were several dogs out there, not just one, and the realization worried her.

Suddenly people came into view beneath her. All were strangers except for Cletus, who stood talking with a tall, black man in a pale gray suit and hat. Except for him, none of the men was dressed up at all. Most wore jeans and T-shirts or work clothes, and many of them had cans of beer in their hands. She watched Cletus and the black man shake hands with a newcomer, a very heavy man Cletus hailed loudly as Howie. At first she couldn't find Joe Miranda; then he came into sight with another man.

132

Both had a net over their shoulders, and the nets were squirming. Yelps were coming out of them.

Dogs! Dogs in nets!

Cissie sucked her breath in as deeply as she could while the nets were lowered down into the pen. Miranda and the other man held the nets by their ends.

"Brujo. Five hundred on Brujo!" cried her Uncle Cletus.

Other men shouted out sums of money, too.

"Six hundred on Raw Jaws," shouted a man in a baseball cap. More offers poured out from the throng below the loft.

"Let 'em loose," bellowed the man Cletus had called Howie.

Then Cissie saw her dog! She saw Spook rolled out of the net! He sprang to his feet and launched himself onto the brown animal, who was just coming out of the other net.

"Cissie, watch it!" Mark's soft, warning whisper was the only sound in the entire barn as the dogfight began.

Spook had begun to growl in the van the moment he heard the barking of the other dogs arriving at the meet. He'd barked defiance at them from inside his cage and struggled to get free to fight them while Howie and Miranda had got him into the net to transport him to the pit.

The Staffordshire Terror

In all the varied and unfamiliar scents of the large barn—the kerosene stink of the lamps, the tobacco and beer smells of the men, and the exciting odors of the seven other dogs—the Staffordshire didn't catch the scent of Cissie. She was too far away from him, and there were too many other smells. He gave all his attention to the brown dog, half-Boxer, half-Samoyed, before him.

The two young dogs crashed together and bounded apart. Then the brown leaped for Spook's throat, missing it by a quarter inch. As he darted past, Spook dived for his left hind leg and caught it in his fangs. Falling to the carpet, the brown dog flailed his body about, jerking free before Spook could get firm hold. Bleeding, the brown one crouched, then sprang for Spook's head. He missed, but as Spook sidestepped him the brown dog's teeth slashed the terrier's side, cutting it open as he went by. In his lust for battle, Spook didn't feel the pain. He whirled about to face his enemy, and this time Spook attacked. He ran, head down, butting the other in the side, bowling him over. Then in a flash Spook had fastened onto the other dog's left ear.

The crowd of men shouted their wild joy while Cissie gasped in horror up in the loft. It was the first sound she'd made.

For a time, with his eyes closed, Spook chewed on his enemy's ear while the other dog struggled.

134

At last the brown dog broke free with the blood from the torn ear half blinding him. Still, the brown animal attacked Spook, getting hold of his right hind leg. Spook twisted his whole body, wrenching his leg away, and went for the brown's side, knocking him to the carpet and fastening onto the right ear this time.

Again the crowd yelled their approval, and the elegantly dressed Leon Gates tapped Joe Miranda on the shoulder and nodded.

Spook held to the brown dog's ear until it managed to rise from the carpet and with all of its strength and bulk buck the terrier off its head. Afterward the brown dog went to a corner of the pen and stood motionless.

Howie, who had refereed many dogfights, shouted, "A turn!"

Cursing, the brown dog's long-shanked owner stepped over the top of the pen, got behind his dog, grabbed him by the collar, and tried to push him forward to attack Spook again. But the brown dog jerked loose from his master. He ran past Spook, who was waiting, and tried unsuccessfully to leap out of the pen. Crashing back, he cowered beside the boards.

Spook didn't attack him. He knew that the brown animal was admitting defeat and instead took one step toward the man who owned the brown dog.

The Staffordshire Terror

The man saw the advance of the Staffordshire and scrambled hastily over the side of the pen while everyone laughed at him.

Howie shouted, "Brujo. The winner is Brujo, the Staffordshire Terror."

According to how they'd bet, men clapped one another on the back, laughing, or they swore. Some collected cash. Others paid it out while Joe Miranda and the brown dog's disappointed owner threw nets over the dogs and carried them out of the blood-spattered pen.

Up in the loft Cissie was weeping softly with her head on Lita's shoulder.

Lita told her over and over in a whisper, "Cissie, he's alive! Spook's okay." She turned to Mark and said, "Let's get out of here now, Mark."

"We can't go, Lita. We have to be last to leave here. I figure there'll be some more dogfights now, but we don't have to watch 'em. We can crawl to the back of the loft and wait there till they're over. Cissie, listen to me. Be *quiet.*"

"He's right, Cissie," urged Lita. "Come on. Don't let anybody hear you crying."

Mark added, "We're going to the police the minute we get out of here, and from there we're going to Miranda's place again. Keep your mind on that, Cissie."

"All right," Cissie told Mark.

* * *

136

Joe Miranda carried the dog he called Brujo not to his own van but to another one, a shining newish green-silver one. Cletus Rose and Deacon Gates, carrying a flashlight, followed Miranda. Gates opened the back doors of the van, and a light went on inside the automobile. The interior of Gates's van had been customized with a built-in cage that slid in and out. Gates opened the bars behind the van doors, and Miranda deposited Spook, net and all, inside. Gates, who had given the flashlight to Cletus, closed the barred doors, then the van doors, and locked them.

Next Gates pulled a wallet from the inside of his coat and counted out ten bills into Joe's hand. "Here, man," he said. "This is to pay for your share of the Staffordshire Terror. Me and Mr. Cletus Rose here, we own this dog together from now on. I take care of him, and I arrange where he fights from now on, okay?"

"That's right," agreed Joe Miranda. "I'm out of it now."

"Yep, that's right," said Cissie's uncle. "We're partners in the dog now, Gates. I never thought I'd be partners with no black man, but Joe says you're okay. You take care of him. I ain't got no place to keep any dog, let alone a fighting one like the Terror. Just you keep me posted on the telephone where he'll be fighting for us, and I'll come and see him and collect my half of what he earns for us."

The Deacon smiled. "I never thought I'd be partners with some white man from Arkansas either, but business is business. That dog can make us plenty of bread, Rose!"

Gates held out his hand, and, after a moment's hesitation, Cletus took it and shook hands with his new partner.

8
The Deacon's Dog

Cissie, Lita, and Mark stayed at the back of the loft while the second, third, and fourth pair of dogs were brought inside to fight. They could hear the bets made and the shouting of the spectators, but none of the three watched or saw one of the dogs killed by another. They only knew that the yelling was different—louder and even more excited.

The noises of automobiles leaving signaled when the meet had at last come to an end. Mark went to the door to look out again. When he came back, he told the girls they'd have to wait another twenty minutes to be sure they could leave safely. While he kept track of time by the lighted dial of his wrist-watch, Cissie crawled across the loft to the spot where she'd watched her dog. It was completely dark below now. The lanterns had been put out and stored, and the pit boards and the carpet and tarpaulin were gone. Except for the three of them, the barn was empty. Joe Miranda's work as host to this meet was over.

"Spook, Spook, I'll save you. I'll rescue you!" she muttered to herself, living over the horrible fight she'd witnessed. It was terrible to think that men would fight dogs deliberately. She hated to see a dogfight any time—or any other kind of animal fight. She didn't even like seeing Darrell wrestle and roll on the ground with the boys he sometimes invited to their place to play.

Mark drove to the sheriff's department on Orange Street, and there he told their story to the officers on duty. Lita and Cissie stood behind him, nodding, while he spoke of the barn near the old-time *asistencia* and of seeing dogs fight in the barn less than an hour before.

Cissie volunteered, "One of the dogs we saw was my terrier, Spook. He was stolen from me by a man named Miranda. We saw my dog at the dogfight and Mr. Miranda, too, along with lots of other men. Mr. Miranda probably took him back to where he lives near Corona. Can we go get my dog now, please?"

The sheriff's officer asked the trio, "You say everybody has left that barn outside Colton?"

"Yes," Lita told him, "but you can tell they were

140

there. The boards and rug are probably still around, and there's dog blood on the boards. I saw it."

"Okay, we'll send cars to look at both places, near Colton and near Corona."

Mark said, "We'll show you how to get to Miranda's."

"All right. You kids go back to your car."

"Sure." Mark led the way out of the big white building, followed by Cissie and Lita.

Lita told Cissie out on the sidewalk, "Miranda and old Cletus could have a big head start on us in Miranda's van. I bet Cletus's car will be gone by the time we get there. I hope it will. Your mom sure doesn't want him to be mixed up in things we talk to others about."

Cissie said bitterly, "He's the cause of all this trouble. I sure hate being careful to keep him out of things."

Lita cut her off. "But it's what your folks want. Remember what I told you. Cletus knows something we don't know. Stella Jane told me plenty, but she didn't tell me what it was."

"Come on, you two!" shouted Mark.

Twenty-five minutes later, Mark's little yellow car and a sheriff's black-and-white one were coming down Dailey Road to Joe Miranda's house.

Mark, the two girls, and two deputies went up

141

to the house and spoke to a very nervous, and soon weeping, Elena Miranda. The six people crowded her small living room.

"My husband's gone away," she told the deputies. "He came home for only a little while, a couple of hours ago, and then he drove away again. He told me to tell his boss that he's quitting his job here. I'm supposed to pack up and take a bus and follow him tomorrow."

"Follow him to where?" asked the deputy.

"Mexico. To the village he came from. He wants to help his brother's family there. They are so poor. They are starving."

Cissie cried, "*Mexico!* He's got my dog with him. He's taking Spook to Mexico!"

A deputy told her sharply, "The border police wouldn't let a dog that looked as if it was used as a fighting animal through. They search the cars that cross over."

Cissie breathed out deeply and went to lean against the front door.

The same deputy then asked Elena Miranda, "Did your husband ever have a dog, a gray terrier, here?"

"Yes, he did." Mrs. Miranda's large brown eyes filled with tears as she looked at Cissie. "But he didn't take the dog away with him tonight. I saw him get the cage he used for the poor dog out of his van and put it in the garage. There was no animal in it."

Cissie cried, "What happened to my dog?"

"I do not know. My husband did not tell me, and I did not ask him. He was in a hurry."

"Let's see your garage," demanded a deputy.

"It is not locked," said Mrs. Miranda.

The sheriff's men, Cissie, Lita, and Mark went out of the house to the garage, where a deputy raised the overhead door. He switched on the inside light. There sat the cage, facing them so they could see its emptiness at a glance. Beyond it was the holding pen, and leaning up against it were some bags labeled *Dog Food*.

Knowing it was useless, Cissie still whistled. One of the deputies turned to look at her. "Well, kids, there was a dog here, but he's gone now."

Mark asked, "Could you get a message to the border to stop Miranda?"

"He's more than likely over into Mexico by now, but we'll give it a try." He put his hand on his hips, looking at the cage and pen, and then shook his head. "You all had better go home now. We'll let you know what happens, if anything does. Are you sure you didn't recognize anybody else at that dog-fight?"

Lita spoke up quickly before Mark could, "No, we didn't."

The same officer asked, "How did you happen to know Miranda?"

Lita told him, "A girl friend of mine told me

somebody she knew told her a Mr. Miranda stole dogs, and my cousin's dog got stolen. My girl friend moved away to Montana, and I don't know where she lives now."

"Okay, miss. If we get a report that there was a dogfight in the Colton area tonight, we'll alert the whole county that somebody's staging fights hereabouts."

"Mr. Miranda was the one who set up the big pen in the barn over in Colton. We watched him do it," said Cissie.

The deputy snorted. "Well, Miranda sure wasn't the only one there, so there may be other men arranging other fights in the future. We might as well leave here now. We haven't got any reason to arrest Miranda's wife." He started back to his car with his partner.

Elena Miranda was standing beside Mark's car. As Cissie got into the back seat, the woman told her softly, "I am sorry. I am sorry. I didn't like what my husband did, but we needed money so badly. We needed it for his brother's children, who are so hungry. Please try to understand. My husband is not a bad man. He is good to his own children."

Cissie could not speak. She turned her head away from the woman, garage, and house as Mark started off.

As they went down Dailey Road behind the black-

and-white car, Mark asked, "Where does your uncle live, Cissie?"

"No! We *can't* go there, Mark."

"Why not? Why didn't you tell the police about him?"

Lita explained, "Because Cissie's mom and dad wouldn't want us to. I don't know why, but they don't."

Mark grunted, then said, "All right, all right. He's the family skeleton, huh, and they want to keep him safe in the closet?"

"That's it, probably," Lita told him. "Let's go home and tell Cissie's folks."

Mark asked sourly, "Are you sure you want to do *that*? They might get mad at me for taking you to a dogfight."

Cissie replied, "I have to tell them about my dog not being at Miranda's tonight, and then I'm going to tell Mr. Cameron, too, on Monday."

With Walt and Shirley Rose and Darrell listening around the big kitchen table, Cissie, Lita, and Mark took turns telling of their adventures that night.

Walt and Shirley Rose kept glancing at one another, and when they heard that Cletus had been present at the fight, Walt reached out to grip his wife's hand. At the end of the story, he asked, "So Spook's disappeared somewhere else now?"

Cissie answered his question. "Yes, Dad. Maybe Uncle Cletus has him now. We didn't tell the deputies about him because Mom said to keep him out of our troubles."

Her father slowly shook his head. "I doubt that he has the dog. Not if Miranda kept Spook at his place all this time. Cletus hasn't got any place to keep Spook. He might have farmed him out to somebody else, though, now that Miranda's gone. That's most likely what he's done. Cissie, how did Spook look when you saw him?"

"Skinny, Dad, but okay to start with. Now he's got a big cut on his side and a bite on the leg."

Cissie's mother said dryly, "Well, I'm sure those will be attended to, if need be, by whoever has him if he's making money as a fighting dog. Your dog will be well looked after as long as he wins." She turned to Mark and said, "Mark, you'd better get on home now. Don't think for a minute that we approve of what you and the girls did tonight. I'd planned to take them to Miranda's tomorrow. You've had a busy night but a dangerous one."

"Sure, Mrs. Rose. I'm sorry. Good night, everybody." Mark got up, looking embarrassed, and went out to his car.

After he'd gone, Shirley Rose turned to Lita and Cissie. "You should be grounded for a long time, both of you, first for going to that barn and then for telling a lie about the movie and not waiting

146

for me. Stop taking matters so much into your own
hands, Lita, and you be careful, Cissie."

"All right, Mom," Cissie said unhappily.

Then Shirley Rose said, "Something happened
here while you were gone. Stella Jane called us.
She's living up in Montana, and she's just fine,
happy as can be."

Lita asked, "Did you tell her about Miranda being
a man?"

"Yes, she sounded surprised. She warned us to be
careful of Cletus and reminded us how he could
hold grudges against folks. She's sure happy to be
away from him."

"That's good news," said Lita.

"Yes, Stella Jane's out of his life. I wish we were,
too." Shirley Rose sighed deeply. "Well, I don't like
what you kids did tonight, but I ought to be glad
you got home safely. And you did learn some things."

At this reminder of Spook Cissie burst into tears.
Miserable, she got to her feet and ran upstairs to
her room, where she flung herself onto her bed.

What she'd learned was just awful. Spook was
still lost to her. He was a prisoner and in danger
every time he fought another dog. Thinking of her
uncle, Cissie clutched at her bedspread, rumpling
it. How she hated having to protect him without
knowing why.

Cissie spent most of Sunday in the swing on the

front porch, refusing to be comforted by any of her family. Though they took turns coming out to ask her if she wanted something to eat or drink or to let her know about a special TV program, she would only shake her head.

As dusk fell, she walked over to the barn, reached up to the nail just inside the door, and took down the collar Spook's mother had worn. She wiped the dust from it with her shirtsleeve and reread the words on the little silver plate, which was much tarnished now. Then she went inside the house and stuffed the collar into the canvas book bag she carried to school.

After thrashing about for a while, Spook untangled himself from the net in which he'd been put inside this new van. He sprang at the bars and at the sides of the moving automobile, but this cage didn't give him his freedom any more than Miranda's homemade one had. The terrier sniffed at its floor and sides. He scented disinfectant, and he also scented dog. Other dogs had been transported in this van. Their scent made his hackles rise.

After a while the movement of the van soothed the dog, so he lay down on the floor and twisted his head over his shoulder to lick at the slash wound on his side. By now it had stopped bleeding and was only oozing a little.

Gates had looked at it quickly and seen that it

would heal in time by itself and not require the services of a veterinarian to sew it shut. Yet he also felt that because of it the terrier should not be fighting for a while. Let the dog get back his strength, but forget about vets. They could be dangerous. They could ask questions about how the dog got hurt. They'd suspect a man of fighting dogs. Possibly if a woman brought the dog in, the way Joe Miranda's wife had done, it would be different. But he wasn't sure.

The Deacon pushed a tape deck into his dashboard so he could have music on his way to the kennel where he always boarded his dogs. Keeping time with the music, tapping his long fingers on the wheel, the Deacon sang, "Baby, baby, baby," along with the tune, as the van traveled westward. Yessir, this dog, this Staffordshire Terror, behind him in the van was some fine animal. Expensive, yes, but a good investment. The dog ought to be a prime moneymaker. An ear dog was hard to beat, better than one that worked the throat or legs. Ear dogs might tear up their opponents, but they didn't cripple or kill them.

An hour and a half later Gates drove up to a wrought-iron gate set in a red-brick wall. Lights in black iron frames were set on each side of the gate. When he honked the van's horn, a fair-haired young man came to the gate with a flashlight. He shone it

on the van, then on Gates's face, nodded, and unlocked the gate to let the car inside. The Deacon
drove along a gravel road, bordered on each side
by lawns and shrubbery that showed up deep green
in his headlights. He took the van in a half circle
behind a large red-roofed, Spanish-style house and
pulled up in a well-lit space before a long, narrow,
stucco building. A redheaded boy came out of the
building to the front of the car to greet Gates with,
"Hi, Deacon. We been expecting you."

Spook had felt the car stop and heard the driver's
door slam shut as Gates got out. He heard the
Deacon and the young man talking; then he heard
the rear door being unlocked and saw the interior
light come on.

Spook crashed onto the bars the instant the van
doors were opened.

"Wow, would you look at him! He sure wants to
get out!" exclaimed the redhead.

Gates said only, "Where's the boss? Where's Bell?"

"Right here, Deacon."

A third person came down the front steps of the
stucco building. He was tall and wore a blue V-
necked sweater and white trousers. Not a young
man, he had a curling brown beard that was streaked
with gray. He walked to the rear of the van, brush-
ing the red-haired boy aside, and peered in at the
plunging terrier. "Have you got any idea what
you have in there, Gates?" he asked.

"A Staffordshire terrier, a thoroughbred, I'd say. That's what I was told."

"A dog's a purebred, not a thoroughbred. Horses are thoroughbreds. But unless I miss my guess, this one's a purebred among purebreds. I've seen gray dogs like this one before."

"Where was that?"

"Come to the house with me after we get this dog into the kennel, and I'll tell you." The bearded man ordered the redheaded boy, "Call Randy at the gate and ask him to come back here. Then get Jim out of the kennel to help you. The way this dog is acting, I don't think you should take him out of the cage at all. Take the whole cage inside the kennel and get him out of it. Then slide the cage back in here. I don't want anybody bitten, and I sure don't want this dog hurt in any way. I want you to give him the finest care at all times. What's he called, Deacon?"

"Brujo."

"Does he answer to that name?"

"I dunno. I doubt it, though. The man I got him from told me over the phone that a family raised him from a pup." Gates laughed. "Maybe they called him Rover."

The bearded man smiled, then asked, "How does he fight?"

"He's an ear dog."

"Good."

"Fat Howie from Calexico called him the Staffordshire Terror tonight when he won."

"That isn't a bad nickname at all. I would never have expected Howie to come up with anything as fancy as that. But as long as the dog's here, we'll name him after you."

Gates touched his chest with his thumb. "After me?"

"Yes, we'll call him the Deacon's dog. That's easier to say. When this dog was a puppy, he probably had a registered name half a mile long, though."

Cissie took the red-leather collar with her to school the following Monday, but she didn't show it to Mr. Cameron immediately. The first thing she did was ask him if she could talk to him and show him something at noon.

"I take it that it has something to do with your dog?" he said. "Did you find out something Saturday, Cissie?"

"Yes." Cissie could only nod because she was afraid she'd start to cry. She added softly, "We found out plenty, Lita and Mark and me. I need to tell you about it."

"Okay, I'll hear you. Come here at twelve-thirty. By that time I'll be through with my lunch."

On the dot Cissie was back at her homeroom to see him, and with her she had the dog collar, which she'd kept all morning in her school locker. Mr.

Cameron pulled a second chair up to his teacher's desk, and he motioned to her to take it. "Okay, Cissie, go ahead."

She looked at him, smiled crookedly, then handed him the red collar without a word.

"Does this belong to your dog? Did you find him?"

"No, it belonged to Spook's mother. Dad and me, we killed her."

"Killed her?" exclaimed Mr. Cameron.

"It was a accident. I'll start at the beginning and tell you the whole story." Cissie's eyes filled with tears, which she wiped away with the tissue he gave her from the box on his desk. She told Mr. Cameron about the accident on the road, about finding the puppy and Stella Jane's elopement, and about Cletus and his rage and Spook's attacking him.

"Well, when we took our cat to the vet in Corona, he told us that Elena Miranda had come there alone and brought him a dog that she said had been mauled by a pack of wild dogs. It died. He believed her story. The vet said that her husband was named Joe and that somebody named Deacon Gates had told her to take the hurt dog to him." Cissie blew her nose and put the tissue carefully into the wastebasket, then took another one. "Lita and Mark and me went out to Joe Miranda's place close to Corona . . ." and Cissie told Mr. Cameron how they had ended up witnessing the dogfight in the barn near Colton. "Oh, it was awful. I saw my dog fight another dog down there." Cissie took another tissue from Cameron's hand.

"What men did you see there, Cissie?"

"My Uncle Cletus, somebody we're pretty sure was Mr. Miranda, and a bunch of other men I never saw before."

"Go on, Cissie. I'm listening."

She told next of going with the sheriff's deputies to Miranda's in hopes of getting Spook back. "But he wasn't there, and neither was Miranda. Oh, he was the right Miranda, all right. But he'd already left. He'd gone down to Mexico, and his wife and kids were going there right away, too. He was taking money he won fighting my dog to help out his brother's poor family there."

The teacher sighed. "I see. Yes, there's terrible poverty down in Mexico in some places. Sometimes, Cissie, something good can come out of something evil, although it's not a system that suits me personally. So you've lost your dog again?"

"It looks that way, doesn't it?"

"Yes, at the moment it does. But we do have some things to work on. This is one of them." He held up the dog collar.

Cissie asked, puzzled, "It wasn't Spook's. What'll we do with that?"

"I think I will ask Kimmie to help us out on this. There are two names on this collar. Fame and Folly.

They could easily be the name of the female dog, and one of them could be the name of her owner or the kennel where she was bred. Anyhow, it might be a lead."

Cissie gripped the seat of the chair as a new thought struck her. "Oh, gosh, the kennel people would make trouble for Dad if they found out our pickup truck hit the female!"

"I doubt that, Cissie. It was an accident."

"But they'd want Spook back if he belongs to them."

Mr. Cameron smiled. "They can't have him any more than you can when you don't know where he is, can they?"

"No, I guess not."

"And you never saw an ad for a lost female Staffordshire terrier, a female with a puppy."

"No, and I watched the papers, too."

"There's something else to tell Kimmie. Those two dogs probably weren't local if there was no newspaper ad for them. They most likely came from some other state or county. Kimmie can look in the out-of-town phone books all over this part of the state for a kennel that has the name Fame or Folly in it. If she finds one, you can call the place on the phone and see what you can learn that might be helpful."

Cissie got up. "Mr. Cameron, do you think I'll ever find my dog?" she asked.

"I sure hope so."

Cissie looked troubled as she said, "Mom doesn't know Dad hit the female dog last year. She doesn't want anybody to know that Dad's brother Cletus is mixed up in this either. Lita and Mark and I didn't tell the sheriff's men about him because Mom wouldn't have wanted us to. And neither does Dad. They'd be plenty mad at me if they knew I'd told you. I just had to tell somebody, though!"

Mr. Cameron asked gently, "Do you have any idea why they're protecting your uncle?"

"No, but he's a bad man, and he's got Dad into trouble in lots of places we've lived. Dad used to be a partner of his in business. Lita and I think he's got something on Dad, something he could do to Dad or tell on him maybe. We don't know what it is, and we don't want to ask Mom. Maybe Mom's just scared of Cletus's coming back to our place and hurting Lita now that Spook's not there to protect us anymore."

"Hmmm." Mr. Cameron was silent a moment. "Does your family own that property out there in Mira Loma?" he asked.

"No, we don't. Dad's the caretaker for Mr. Benson, who lives in town. That was where Mr. Benson grew up. His folks owned the ranch."

"I know Benson. He manages one of the savings banks in town. Well, Cissie, you'd better get on to your next class. Keep your hopes up." Mr. Cameron took the dog collar from his desk and handed it to her. "Here, this is yours. Keep it in your locker. I'll let you know if Kimmie comes up with anything. If she does, we'll want to have that collar handy."

Cameron was scowling as his class filed in for the afternoon. He didn't like betting. That was one of the chief reasons he'd quit boxing. Men had bet on him, and it had made him feel like an animal, not a human being. They had urged him to turn professional, but he hadn't felt like beating out his brains so they could make money on him.

Quitting and going to college to become a teacher when he might have become a rich and famous boxer had been a sacrifice. But he hadn't regretted it for a moment. He liked teaching. He liked kids, and he hated to see one as down as this little Cissie Rose was. He made up his mind to take more of a hand in Cissie's troubles.

9
The Kennel Men

Thursday morning Mr. Cameron asked Cissie to remain a minute after class. Then he said to her, "Kimmie had some luck yesterday looking in phone directories for dog breeders. There's a Fame Kennel in Los Angeles that breeds Staffordshire terriers. The ad said that a Mr. Gordon owns it and that his dogs are supposed to be famous blue-ribbon show dogs."

"*Spook?*" Cissie's eyes grew very wide. "A *show* dog?"

"Perhaps he might have been. You ought to call this kennel as soon as you can. Try to talk to Mr. Gordon."

"What'll I tell him?"

"Tell him about the red collar you have. Maybe he can tell you something about it."

Cissie sighed. "I suppose I'll have to tell him about Dad's hitting the female dog and that her puppy's grown up and been stolen from us and is a fighting dog now."

"Well, perhaps you won't have to tell him that all at once. If the dead female was his, I have a hunch that he'll come out here to Riverside to talk to you about her. Staffordshire terriers are very valuable dogs, remember?"

"I remember. Okay, I'll call him, but if he does come out, where will I see him? He can't come to my home, because Mom doesn't know about Dad hitting the female."

Mr. Cameron nodded and said, "Here at school at noon. You may use my room."

"Will you be here, too?"

"Do you want me to be, Cissie?"

"I sure do. Oh, Mr. Cameron, I'm not sure about calling up somebody I don't even know."

"Lots of people feel timid about contacting people who are strangers to them, but when they have to do it, they do it. There are a lot of things in life that we don't want to do. Every time we do one of them we get a little bit stronger ourselves."

He hoped his pep talk would give Cissie some courage, because this was something she really should do. She certainly looked small and forlorn now, a far different girl from the first day she had come into his class. He remembered how he'd given her an *A* on the paper she wrote about her dog and how she'd defended the dog's ability as a fighter. Poor Cissie.

She burst in, interrupting his thought. "I didn't tell Dad about talking to you about Uncle Cletus. Would I have to tell Mr. Gordon about my uncle?"

"I don't see offhand that you need to, Cissie."

"Then I won't. If Mr. Gordon comes here, I'll just tell him about Joe Miranda taking Spook and how Miranda's gone to Mexico and how he probably got rid of my dog to somebody else, somebody I don't know."

"That ought to do it, Cissie. Be sure tomorrow that you bring that picture of Spook you had taken for the report."

That night Lita gave Cissie all the coins she had, and the next day at noon Cissie went across the street from her school to the pay phone at the supermarket and got the operator to call the Fame Kennel in Los Angeles and ask for the owner, Mr. Gordon.

He was there, according to the operator. Cissie put quarter after quarter and then some dimes into the slot at the top of the phone. Finally she squeaked, "Hello, this is Cissie Rose in Riverside. Is Mr. Gordon there, the Mr. Gordon who raises terriers?"

"Yes, this is Gordon speaking. What can I do for you?"

Cissie's hopes rose. He had a nice, soft voice. She

told him, "I've got a red-leather dog collar that says *Fame*'s *Folly* on it. Would it belong to you?"

"If it has those words on it, it would, I suspect." There was excitement in the man's voice. "You've got my dog then? The female? What about her pup?"

Cissie told him, "No, I haven't got either of them, just the red collar." She hesitated. "I saw both of 'em, though."

He said, "A female Staffordshire and her male pup were stolen from my kennel last year. You say you've got her collar but not the dog or the pup either?"

"That's right."

"But do you know where they are or what happened to them?"

Cissie's voice broke. "Oh, Mr. Gordon, could you come out here to Riverside tomorrow at noon? It's a long story. I'm at a pay phone with no more money to feed it. Would you come to my school so I can tell you what I do know?"

The man was silent for a moment. Then he said, "All right. I'll come. At noon, you say? Where is this school?"

Cissie gave the name of her school, its location, and the number of Mr. Cameron's room. Then she said, "Good-bye, Mr. Gordon," and hung up.

She'd done it and it hadn't been too bad, but tomorrow she'd see Spook's true owner face to face. That *could* be bad.

* * *

Mr. Gordon was quite an elderly man with a suntanned face, bright blue eyes, and white hair. He was of medium height, he was wearing a green tweed jacket, and he smiled warmly at Cissie after he'd shaken hands with Mr. Cameron.

"So you're Cissie Rose?" he said. "You're the one who has the information about my gray terriers?"

"I'm not sure. How do you do?" asked Cissie politely. Then she said, "Even if I haven't got the dogs, I have the dog collar the mother had on, and I've got the picture of the puppy when he was almost grown up."

Mr. Gordon sat down in the chair Mr. Cameron had ready for him. "Let's see them, please."

Cissie said, "Mr. Cameron has them in his desk drawer."

Mr. Cameron opened the drawer and took out the things Cissie had given him to keep for her.

Gordon looked first at the collar. He frowned as he said, "Yes, this is Folly's collar, all right. Now, Cissie, tell me what happened to her and the pup?"

"I'm sorry, but she's dead, Mr. Gordon." Cissie paused and sighed, then went on. "Our truck hit her when she wouldn't get out of our way on the road. Dad thought she was a coyote."

"Oh, that's bad! That's too bad! I'd hoped I'd find her, but I guess I shouldn't be too surprised." Mr. Gordon spoke with a sigh. "Folly didn't know

162

much about cars, I'm afraid. She was always in the kennel or in a car going to a dog show. She didn't have any experience of highways. What about Fortune, her puppy? His real name, in case you'd like to know, is Sir Fortune of Castlehaven."

"Sir Fortune of Castlehaven?" Cissie shook her head in amazement. "I kept him when I couldn't find out who owned him. There never were any ads from anybody saying they'd lost two gray terriers. I called him Spook because he was such a pale gray. Then he got stolen from our home. I don't know where he is now, but some bad men were fighting him against other dogs."

The kennel owner shook his head. He said angrily, "That's terrible, blast it! His being a Staffordshire would make him very attractive for that purpose! I imagine he's been bitten and mauled by now so he could never be shown at a dog show. It makes me sick when I hear about dogs fighting. To think of one of my show dogs being used that way is even worse."

Although her words choked her, Cissie cried, "Mr. Gordon, I know he isn't really mine. If I ever find Spook, I'll give him back to you."

"No." Gordon shook his head. "No, you keep him if you ever find him. He's been raised in a family and needs human company now. I wouldn't be able to show him with my other dogs, so I give him to you. But if you find him and breed him, breed

163

him only to another purebred Staffordshire terrier.
Then call me when the puppies are born. I might
want to buy them."

"I promise. I sure do!" Spook was truly hers now,
but where *was* he? Then Cissie asked, "How come
your two dogs were way out in the country where
we live? How come they were so far away from their
kennel? Didn't you ever advertise in the papers here
about getting them back?"

As Mr. Gordon got up, he told Cissie, "Yes, I did
advertise, but not in the papers here. I thought,
mistakenly it turns out, the dogs might have been
taken north of L.A., so I advertised in papers all
the way up to San Francisco. As to why they were
out here, I think I may know.

"I had to fire a kennel man last year for not keeping my dog runs as clean as I like them. I didn't
know at first that he was a confirmed drunkard, or
I would never have hired him. The same night I
fired him, or so I was told by people who knew him,
he got drunk and said he planned to get even with
me for letting him go. Folly and her puppy turned
up missing the very next morning, and I think he
stole them. He knew he couldn't sell them to other
dog breeders because they would be recognized. So,
to spite me, it appears that he let my dogs out of his
car alongside some little-traveled road near Riverside and abandoned them.

"We'll never know the whole truth about it,

though. I later learned that my former employee died not long after the dogs were stolen." Gordon picked up the photo of Spook for a second glance, then put it down. "This is a fine-looking animal. You did a good job raising him. Did you train him, too?"

"I tried to, but I didn't do so good. All Spook really knows is how to fight, I guess. I'll take him to obedience school if I ever find him again."

Mr. Gordon's face darkened. He said warningly, "Cissie, you may not want him when and if you can get him back. He might have changed a great deal. I don't mean only in appearance. I know Stafford-shires. He might not be friendly to you anymore. Fighting could have changed him."

"No, Spook won't change! He never would! I don't care what he looks like or how beat up he is, he'll still be my dog!"

"I surely hope so, my dear. Well, I am glad to meet you and solve the mystery of Folly and Fortune, but I ought to be getting back to Los Angeles." The owner of the Fame Kennels reached into his pocket and pulled out a little white business card, which he gave to Cissie. "This has my address and phone number on it. Now will you give me Folly's collar to take back with me, please? I'd like to have it as a remembrance of her."

"Sure, Mr. Gordon. It was yours all along. You'll hear from me when I find Spook."

"Yes, I'd like to know about him. Thank you."
Cissie watched as he took the collar, then she said
to Mr. Cameron, "Poor Spook. He's sure had a hard
life."

The long, roomy, very clean, wire-walled kennel
Spook was kept in was bound to be more to any
healthy dog's liking than the pen Joe Miranda had
made. But accustomed from puppyhood to the
friendly company of a family and to having other
animals besides dogs around him, Spook didn't take
to his new environment. When he wasn't eating or
sleeping, he prowled the length of this big, airy
cage, padding back and forth, back and forth. There
were no dogs nearer to him than five cages away,
and those animals were females, no fighting chal-
lenge to the Staffordshire.

The young men who helped run the kennel near
Santa Barbara were responsible for Spook's feeding,
but they never spoke to him. Nor did Mr. Bell, the
brown-bearded older man, though he came very
often to look at the terrier.

Sometimes Deacon Gates came with Bell. Though
the sight of the kennel man brought forth no interest in Spook, the hair on his neck and shoulders
rose at the sight of Gates because somewhere dimly
in Spook's brain there was a coupling of this man
with Miranda and the hated electric prod.

Too, Gates snapped his fingers to annoy the terrier. One afternoon when he did so, Spook started walking stiff legged toward him.

Gates spoke to the dog, "You don't know it, baby, but we sure have a fight lined up for you next weekend in San Burdoo. You'll be fighting against one of the top dogs on the West Coast."

Bell kept his eyes on Gates as he said, "Deacon, if your dog wins this match, we ought to think about matching him against some pit bulldogs on the East Coast. We could fly him back there."

"Naw, not yet, Bell." The Deacon frowned, then told the other, "The fat old dude who owns this dog half-and-half with me, old Cletus Rose, don't want to let him out of his sight. He wants him to fight on this coast so he can travel around to watch the matches. He says he runs a auto-repair shop, but I don't go there. I might get my clothes dirty."

Bell laughed. "I wouldn't expect you to do that. All right. Buy this dog from him soon as you can."

"I plan to, baby, when I can. I'll make the old dude an offer for him."

"Buy him right after this next fight."

"I can't. I haven't got the bread."

"Don't worry about that. I'll lend you the money if the dog wins his match. Later on we'll work out a partnership arrangement together."

"That suits me. I'm short of money just now. I had bad luck with a couple of horses last week, and then I dropped some in a card game, too."

167

"Those things happen. Then it's settled? After the next match, if this dog wins, I'll set it up with my friend here to have you and me and this dog flown back East. They'll arrange for matches for him back there."

"You bet it's settled, far as I'm concerned, baby. No sweat. I'll ask old Cletus Rose to name his price. It'll be high."

"You know, I don't understand that dude. He takes the dog personally, if you know what I mean, like it was a person more than a pooch. Sometimes he seems to hate it. He likes to think how beat up it'll get from fighting. I don't think he'd grieve if the dog got killed in a match, even if it cost him a chunk of money."

Bell replied, "Deacon, that's all the more reason to get this dog away from him as fast as you can. That's no attitude for a businessman to have. You and I want this dog to win and to keep on winning for us. I know for a fact that the bets run high in the East and even higher down South. I could fix it so we got part of the gate, too, in some places this dog would fight. How does that suit you?"

"It suits me just fine, baby. Just fine. That old Cletus Rose as a partner don't do nothing for me but give me a sour stomach."

The following Friday night Mr. Cameron took pretty soft-eyed Kimmie out to supper at a place they'd never gone to before. It was located in a cellar under another restaurant.

Both of them decided they didn't like the place. It was crowded and noisy, and Kimmie complained that the meal tasted of cigarette smoke.

When the check came at last, she stood up, laughed, and said, "I'm going to fix my makeup and then make a real short phone call to my sister Claire, Perry, to see how her croupy baby is doing. Will you be all right while I'm gone?"

"Oh, sure. Nothing is going to come in here and get me. Go on, Kimmie. Get more beautiful and tell Claire I hope the baby's okay."

He sat back in his chair, waiting, drumming his fingers on the table. From past experience he knew he was stuck with at least ten to fifteen minutes of blaring music, smoke, and his own thoughts.

Five minutes went by, and during that time two men came out of the barroom to sit down at the little table next to his. They ordered highballs and at once began to talk, ignoring his presence. It seemed to Perry, who listened because he had nothing else to do, that they were both a bit drunk because their words were slurred and their voices overloud.

He paid little heed to their conversation about horses and various racetracks until one asked, "Are you goin' to the matches tomorrow night, Phil?"

"What matches?"

"The dogfights. I got a phone call today about 'em."

Mr. Cameron became alert at once. He'd heard somewhere that this was a restaurant favored by the gambling and sporting crowd, but until now he'd forgotten that bit of information. This conversation might be interesting. His mind went at once to Cissie Rose.

"Where are the matches gonna be this time? In that old barn again?" the bigger man asked. "I couldn't go there last time, but I was there a year ago."

"No, not at the barn. At the old roadhouse on Green Spot Road outside San Burdoo. They're gonna take up around nine o'clock. I hear tell there'll be some real fine dogs there. I *was* at the barn, and I saw a fancy gray dog fight. The Staffordshire Terror, they called him. That dog's a natural-born fighter. He's going to be on the bill tomorrow night, and he's worth seeing, lemme tell you. The other dogs are sure scared of him, and they got cause to be. Them Staffordshires are something!"

"Yeah. Well, I'll try to go."

"You won't be sorry."

"Are you going?"

"Yep. I plan to bet heavy on that gray dog."

"Who handles him?"

"I only know his half-owner, Deacon Gates. He's

170

the fancy-dressing black man you see a lot around the meets."

"Yeah, I see him at the racetrack, too. I know who he is."

"Well, he don't board the dog hereabouts. He brings him to the meet in his van. If you want to get a look at the dog before he fights, you might ask Gates to let you see him in the van before he gets put into the net. That's what I do. I like to look at the dogs the way I look at horses before they race. You can tell about their spirit that way."

"You're right. But lots of folks drive vans. What does this guy's look like so I'll know it from the others?"

"I was told that it's a sort of greenish-silver color, and it ain't so old as most of them."

"Okay, thanks for the tip. Let's have another drink. Hey, waitress, over here!"

Perry Cameron had caught every word, listening with mounting excitement. This gray dog was Cissie's animal. He was sure it was. Deacon Gates was the name of the man who'd sent Elena Miranda to the Corona vet. Yes, it was Cissie's dog.

Kimmie came back at the same time the men's drinks arrived. Mr. Cameron rose, took her by the elbow, and said, "Let's get out of here, honey. I have to take you home. Something's come up, and I have to go someplace tonight."

"What came up? What's wrong, Perry? You never did this before!" Suddenly she flared, "Is it some other girl?"

He smiled down at her. "Trust me. No, I have to see a man about a dog."

Walt and Shirley Rose were alarmed to see headlights coming down the old Benson Road toward their place. It couldn't be Mark because he was already there, out on the back porch practicing some new dance steps with Lita while the radio blared music for them. No one else was expected.

Cissie was up in her room, trying to get into a new book from the library, but instead she was moping over Spook. Darrell was gluing a model airplane together in the kitchen, smelling up the whole house.

Shirley Rose got up from watching the news on TV and said to her husband, "Walt, somebody's coming here!"

"Yeah, I saw the lights, too." He reached under the sofa he sat on and dragged out his rifle. "I'll be ready for him, whoever he is, and if he's come here to make trouble he'll get more than he expected. It might be Cletus."

Mrs. Rose was peeking anxiously through the curtains. She said all at once, "It isn't him this time, Walt, not unless he's got a new car."

From where she lay on her bed, Cissie heard the

172

car drive up. Wondering who it was, she went to her window to look down below.

When her dad switched on the front-porch light, she recognized the man in the car at once. Mr. Cameron! Her teacher *here* at *her* house!

She watched him get out and go around the front of his car to meet her father, who had just stepped down off the front porch. Cissie gasped. Her dad had his rifle held ready across his chest.

His words terrified her. "Whoever you are, don't you take one step nearer. We don't welcome black folks here. Who are you and what do you want from me?"

"Mr. Rose, you don't need that rifle. I'm Perry Cameron, Cissie's teacher from the middle school. Can I talk to you privately?" Cameron's classroom tone carried very well, so well that Cissie, who had been gasping with fright and now with embarrassment, heard each word distinctly from the upstairs window.

"My girl's teacher, huh? She said he was named Cameron," replied Walt Rose, "but I sure didn't know he was a black man. She never told me."

Mr. Cameron answered, "No, I can see by my reception here that Cissie didn't tell you. Well, she does have a black teacher, and I'm he."

"Okay, okay, so you're him, but what did you come out here for? What do you want from us? Is my girl in trouble at school maybe?"

"No, she's a good student. It isn't that, but I do have to talk to you privately about something."

Cissie let out a sigh of relief. Spook! It had to be about her dog. Mr. Cameron seemed to be getting more and more interested in Spook and her.

Privately, but that wasn't fair of Mr. Cameron at all. An instant later Cissie had one leg over the windowsill, then the other, and was crawling as quietly as she could along the roof to a place just above the overhang of the front porch. She lay flat on the shingles there, listening, hoping she hadn't missed much of the conversation going on below her.

Her father was talking, sounding more friendly now, "So, Cameron, you're sure about the time and place?"

"Yes, I'm sure. I think that the gray Staffordshire terrier on the fight bill tomorrow night is your daughter's dog. He's supposed to be driven there in a silver-green van, owned by a black man. It's my strong hunch that the dog inside it will be Cissie's. I figured that you might want to go and see for yourself what's going on with her animal. You could call the police from somewhere nearby, then be outside waiting for them to show up."

Cissie clutched at a shingle, straining to hear what her father would say.

"Let me think about it for a minute, Cameron. You know, I'd sure like to put a smile on Cissie's

174

face again. I haven't seen her smile for weeks. I guess I will go."

"Well then, you be there in San Burdoo tomorrow night at the place I told you about, near nine o'clock, and you could be in luck where that gray dog's concerned. You won't have any trouble finding the old roadhouse."

"Thanks for telling me about this, Cameron."

"I'm glad I could do it. I don't like seeing Cissie so unhappy. Okay, Rose, I'll be going now. Better not tell your family about this. Keep it to yourself. It isn't a thing for your wife and kids to worry over."

"No, it sure ain't," Cissie's father said. Then he added, "You know, I'm glad Cissie's got a teacher who takes so much interest in her. She sure praises you to the skies. I won't tell anybody why you came out here, but you tell me something now. What am I going to tell my wife? She spotted you coming, and I'm danged sure she's got her eye on you and me right now through the living-room curtains. You'd better come in and have some coffee with us so it'll look like you were in the neighborhood and just dropped in. If you don't, Shirley'll ask me questions all night, and so will anybody else who saw you."

"Yes, I see what you mean. All right, lead the way."

Cissie slid backward along the shingles until she

found a place wide enough to turn around to crawl back through her bedroom window. Being out on the roof had dirtied her shirt and jeans something terrible. They were too soiled to wear downstairs without her mother asking what she'd been doing to get them so filthy. Hastily Cissie peeled them off and, opening her closet, grabbed a fresh shirt and clean pants and jammed her bare feet into her sandals.

By the time her mother had called, "Cissie, we have company," twice, she was almost ready to go down.

One look at herself in her dresser mirror told her that there wasn't any dirt from the roof on her face and hair. She spoke happily to her reflection, "Okay now, girl, you watch your step. Act cool. Don't let Dad or Mr. Cameron catch on that you eavesdropped on what they said just now, or they'll both get mad at you." She grinned joyously at her reflection. "Golly, I might have Spook back by tomorrow night. Oh, Spook, Dad'll get you and bring you home to me for sure if he can!" She went out of her room and down the stairs into the living room where everybody else had gathered.

Mr. Cameron, who was all dressed up in a dark gray jacket and slacks, was sitting on the little sofa next to Lita while the others sat on chairs or hassocks. Cameron and Mark were deep in talk about basketball and which teams were the best teams in the country. Lita was beaming, and Darrell was staring open-mouthed at the black teacher he'd heard so much about. Mrs. Rose was smiling and Walt Rose listening in interest to Mark and Mr. Cameron.

"Hey," Cissie put in very brightly, hoping she sounded surprised, "this is sure neat, Mr. Cameron, having you come visit us!"

"Well, I was out this way, so I decided it would be nice to drop in on you," he replied. A pretty good actor, he smiled warmly. "But don't you tell the other kids at school, or they'll get scared I might pop in on them at any time."

"I sure won't tell anybody."

"You're welcome to drop in anytime," said Shirley Rose, before she started for the kitchen to put on the coffee.

A moment later, though, she was back in the room to interrupt the talk of basketball with, "Oh, Cissie, your dad must have forgot to bring in the bag of sugar from today's grocery shopping. Will you get it, please? It's still out in the truck."

"Okay, Mom."

Reluctant to leave, but not wanting to be disobedient, Cissie hurried out the front door to the old pickup. There wasn't any sack of sugar in the front seat, so it had to be in the bottom of the truck in the back. She climbed up into it over the tailgate and rummaged around in the heap of towrope, toolboxes, and spare tires. No white paper sack there. Then she lifted the old paint-stained tarpaulin her dad used to protect grocery sacks from the weather. There was the sugar, lying flat on its side the way it had fallen out of the grocery bag when he'd carried it in.

Holding the five-pound bag under one arm, Cissie stood for a moment in the bottom of the truck. She was still holding one end of the tarpaulin in her right hand. It was pretty heavy canvas, and it was large, too. Big enough, you bet!

All at once she grinned and nodded.

10
The Roadhouse

Mr. Benson came to inspect his property the next morning. He was a short, stout man with waving gray hair, a square face, steel-rimmed spectacles, and a bright-pink complexion. As he always did, he walked over his land with Walt Rose, but this time Cissie went with them because Benson had asked her to. He said he wanted this "pretty little girl" to accompany them, and she soon learned why. He belonged to a group of people who were very interested in the public schools of the state. He wanted to ask her questions about what she was being taught and how much homework she had. She told him what she could.

Then she asked him a question, "Mr. Benson, do you know my teacher, Mr. Perry Cameron? He says he knows you."

"Sure, I know Perry. I've known his family for years. They're one of the real old black families in town. He used to be a sort of harum-scarum kid, but I hear he settled down later on and then went to college when he got out of the Navy. He's got fine parents. I've known them and done business with them for a long, long time. What does he teach?"

"English, Mr. Benson. He gives lots of homework and wants a lot of reports written, but he's good. You know he really cares about us kids. My cousin Lita and her boyfriend had him in school, too. They liked him as much as I do."

Walt Rose added, "Yes, Cameron came here visiting us just last night. I took a liking to him, though at first I wasn't sure. We never had a Negro guest before. Cissie told her mother that she had a black teacher, but nobody ever told me. I wish they had. I met him with a rifle."

"Did you? Well, I'm glad it turned out all right in the end, Rose. You know, I didn't realize that teachers made home visits anymore."

"They don't," Cissie muttered under her breath, as she lagged behind the men.

Mr. Benson's voice floated back to her, though he didn't turn around. "Say, Rose, let's try something on this property that my father used to do. He used to grow potatoes. You could do some farming here, not just keep things in repair. We ought to get that old tractor running instead of letting it rust away in the shed. I think we might plant this field to spuds and get some good results out of it. The farmers in Perris make a good crop most years. This county grows pretty good potatoes."

Cissie wasn't listening to the men discuss potatoes. Her eyes, as she trailed them, were focused on the Rose's battered old pickup truck parked next to the house. She was grinning as she tromped along, now and then pulling up a tumbleweed by its roots. She wondered if her dad's mind was really on potatoes or, like hers, on what he planned to do that night!

Walt Rose told his wife that he had to go into town that Saturday evening to get the new chain saw Mr. Benson had neglected to bring out that morning. He said that Benson had asked him to come to his house in Riverside for it, so it could be put into use Monday morning to cut down the pepper tree that had rotted out on the inside. The tree was going to split when the next windstorm came, and it could fall on the house. Or honeybees or skunks or opossums could decide at any moment that the hollow tree would make a nice home.

Cissie wanted to grin as she listened to her father talk about the chain saw. Part of what he said was true. She had heard Mr. Benson say that he'd forgotten the chain saw after he and her dad had talked about spuds. But he'd also said there wasn't any big rush for it and to pick it up anytime in the next six weeks. The chain saw was only her dad's excuse to get away. When he told his fib at the table, Cissie kept her eyes on her plate.

She didn't watch TV that night with the others. She said she wanted to go upstairs to read the book of ghost stories she'd got out of the school library.

Lita was painting her fingernails to get ready for a date with Mark that night. "Go ahead," she said to Cissie. "Scare the daylights out of yourself."

"Boo," muttered Darrell. Then he stuck his fingers in his ears and waggled them.

As Cissie left the room after sticking her tongue out at him, Shirley Rose said softly to Lita, "I think Cissie's snapping out of her sadness over her dog at last. Maybe she's decided it's a lost cause and will ask us to take her to the pound for a new puppy."

"I got the feeling she was feeling better today, too," said Walt Rose.

"I sure hope so." Lita sighed. "Boo's better than boohoo any day. She can't go on this way, or it'll make an old lady out of her. I'm glad she's up there reading."

Cissie wasn't reading or about to read. She'd finished the ghost book long ago. She went upstairs, changed her flimsy sandals for tennis shoes, got her bright-green windbreaker out of her closet, put it on, and climbed out her bedroom window. Getting to the ground was easy, because just before dark she'd placed the ladder from the tool shed between her window and Lita's under the old pepper tree, where it wouldn't be spotted.

She went to the pickup truck, climbed up over the fender, and got into the truck bottom. Then she lifted the tarpaulin and crawled under it, covering herself with it completely. It was too early for her dad to come out of the house and start on his way to San Burdoo, but when he did, he'd be carrying some freight he hadn't expected along with him. She would be too light a load for him to sense that the rear of the truck wasn't empty as he drove.

If he got Spook back tonight, she planned to be there to claim her dog. Maybe other folks couldn't handle him after he'd been fighting, but she was sure she could. She just knew she could! Mr. Gordon hadn't scared her by what he'd said about the possibility of Spook's changing. Oh, he knew a lot about dogs, about Staffordshires in particular, but he didn't know Spook Rose!

It had been just after one o'clock that afternoon when the Deacon drove his van through the wrought-iron gates of Mr. Bell's estate and behind the big house to the kennels at the rear.

He found Bell inside the kennels along with two of his young helpers. He was holding a lean, black Doberman while she was being groomed by the young men. Bell reached into his shirt pocket and

gave Gates one of the long, brown miniature cigars
he had there.

As the Deacon lit it, he asked Bell, "Are you
takin' some of your dogs to the meet tonight?"

"Yes, I plan to take two of my females in my van.
I'm bringing Gay Lady here and Apple Pie, the
biscuit-colored Boxer."

"How are they doin' these days?"

"Gay Lady's won a fight up the coast, but Apple
Pie's new at the game. Still, I think she's got the
makings of a terror, too, even if she's not a Staffordshire like your dog."

Gay Lady jumped down at command from the
grooming table and was led away by one of the
youths. In a moment the same kennel helper came
back with the female Boxer and lifted her to the
grooming table with the words, "Here she is, Mr.
Bell."

"This is Apple Pie," Bell explained to the
Deacon, as he patted her on the head. "Say, Gates,
how have things been going for you lately? Are you
winning or losing?"

The black man shrugged. "I win a little; I lose
a little. I can't complain, but I can't brag neither."

"Is our deal still on to buy the gray terrier if he
wins tonight?"

"As far as I'm concerned, it is."

"Have you tried to buy out your partner yet?"

"I called him two days back and asked him what

he wanted, but he didn't give me a figure. He said he'd think about it and wanted me to call him back today."

"And did you call him this morning?"

"I tried to before I left with my van, but nobody answered the phone."

"Call him from here. Call him from the house when we're through exercising your animal."

"Okay, I got his number. I planned to do it later on or see him at the match, but I'll try it again now."

Apple Pie was groomed in short order and a spiked collar put around her neck, too. Then she was led back to her kennel.

The Deacon asked Bell, "Are you goin' to groom the Terror, too?"

"No, he was hosed down in his cage early this morning, so he's clean, and he's already got a collar on. He's too much of a handful to groom like Gay Lady and Apple Pie. What we have to do is exercise him on the treadmill. Do you want to see him? After all, he's your animal. Afterward we'll go to the house so you can make that phone call."

Moments later Gates and Bell were in front of Spook's cage, and the dog was waiting for them, growling. He'd not only heard their voices as they approached, he'd caught their scent and had not forgotten Gates.

Looking in at the dog, Gates said with a chuckle,

"He's in good form. Ready to tear up anything that comes his way. How are you gonna get him outa there and onto the treadmill? Joe Miranda used to do that with an electric prod."

"So do we. Come on now, boys. What's keeping you?"

Bell's helpers, who had gone on ahead, came through a side door, carrying a wooden treadmill, which they set down before the cage. One went back and returned with a leather muzzle and a leash, and the other produced a wandlike prod and heavy leather gauntlets.

"Okay, it's Peter's turn to go in," said Bell, "unless"—he turned to look at Gates—"unless *you* want to muzzle the dog?"

"Not me! Not me!" Gates waved his hands in the air, laughing.

Spook, excited, threw himself against the bars, barking and snarling.

Fair-haired Peter drew on the gauntlets and took the muzzle and prod. When the other young man opened the cage door for him, he stepped swiftly inside. Spook lunged immediately, not at him but at the closing door. His eyes were intent on Gates.

"Get him, Peter," shouted Bell. "Don't let him out." Peter, a strongly built young man, flung himself onto Spook from the rear, grabbing hold of the back of his collar. While the dog reared and plunged, Peter, who had no need of the prod now, rammed the muzzle over the terrier's jaws. Then, forcing Spook down by sheer strength, he fastened the muzzle by its straps.

"Okay, do the rest now," ordered Bell. He looked at Gates and said, "He surely would like to find out what you taste like. He remembers your teasing him."

"I know. I know. I got his message."

Gates and Bell stood back as Spook, now on the leash, came out of the cage and was alternately dragged and prodded onto the treadmill where he was made to walk. Though he exercised steadily, Spook's head was turned toward Gates, and low growls came constantly through the stout muzzle he wore.

"Personally, I don't hold with the muzzling," Bell told Gates. "I think after a time it hurts a dog's spirit. I like the net better at the matches. The audience likes to see the dogs struggle in them and watch them get unrolled to fight."

"Yeah, Miranda didn't go in for muzzles, neither."

After watching Spook for another minute, Bell told Gates, "All right, let's go to the house now so you can make that phone call."

Five minutes later the elegant Gates was dialing from a telephone in Bell's book-lined study. The Deacon gazed at Bell, who was sitting in a deep chair, looking at the photograph gallery on his wall.

The photos were all of dogs Bell had owned, some pet dogs, but mostly fighting dogs. Bell had shown him the pictures the first time he'd come to his house to board a dog.

The phone began to ring in Cletus Rose's apartment, and then the Deacon heard a hoarse, rasping voice say, "Hello, who's this?"

"Hey, Rose, is that you? It's me, Leon Gates, callin' you back like you asked me to."

"Oh, yeah, Gates."

"Have you made up your mind about sellin' your half of that dog to me?"

"I guess I have. I might as well sell him. I think mebbe I'll go back to Arkansas where I come from. I got lots of family back there. I don't see myself takin' no mean-as-hell dog with me in my car."

"Okay. What do you want for your half then?"

"How about six thousand dollars?"

"Six thousand, huh? That's pretty steep for a pooch." Gates's eyes were on Bell, who had turned around in his chair to watch him.

"I won't take a dime less, Gates."

"You say you won't take a dime less than six thousand?" the Deacon repeated, so Bell could hear what Cletus had said.

Bell asked softly, "Six, is it?"

Gates nodded.

Bell nodded, too.

188

"Okay, Rose," Gates told him. "If the dog wins his match tonight, I'll pay you six thousand."

"He'll win," promised Cletus. "See you at the match. Be sure you bring the money in cash. So long, Gates."

Cletus hung up, and a second later so did the Deacon.

Gates told Bell, "He wants the bread in cash."

"That's all right. I figured he would. I've got it ready." Bell got up. "I'll bring it with me tonight and give it to you when the dog wins. Let Rose think you own the dog all alone now."

"Sure, why not? I won't mind getting shed of that fat old dude. Let him go back to Arkansas."

Bell smiled. "I hope to be heading East before he will. Could you go back to the Carolinas with me early next week, Deacon? I've got my friend with the private plane standing by to fly us there with any of my dogs that win matches tonight."

"I guess I could close down operations for a while here." Gates was grinning. "I guess the females don't need cages, but have you got one for the Terror?"

"Yes, I had another dog like him some years back, another Staffordshire. I had a special lightweight cage made for him."

"What happened to him? That musta been before I started bringin' my dogs to board here."

189

The Staffordshire Terror

"It was. I had to shoot him after a match because he was so badly injured."

Gates answered, "Too bad . . . Yeah, I had that happen, too. My dog woulda lived, but she wouldn't ever have fought for me again. I couldn't see wasting money to feed her and board her, so I shot her. I made a lot of money with that dog. It was real bad luck for me when she couldn't fight anymore."

Bell nodded.

After he'd talked with Gates, Cletus Rose dropped the phone receiver into its cradle and went to sit in his armchair. He rubbed his chin with his fist.

He was lonesome. It wasn't an easy thing for him to admit, but he missed Stella Jane. He missed her home cooking and her cleaning up, and he missed her company, too. She had never said much and kept to her room a lot, but having her around had been a comfort to him.

"A man needs some comfort in life," he mumbled to himself, as he got up and went to the refrigerator for a beer.

The refrigerator was almost empty now that he had to eat his meals in cafés, something he didn't enjoy. After pulling the tab on the top of the beer can, Cletus went back to his chair. He was scowling as he put the can onto the table next to him. Maybe he should have asked Gates for $8,000, just to see if he would go that high. Well, it was too late now.

Cletus sensed somehow that this man wasn't the sort of guy you raised a price on once you'd agreed to it. Black or not, he made Cletus feel uneasy, a little scared. The price would have to stay at $6,000.

Well, $6,000 wasn't bad at all, not for a dog that hadn't cost him anything more than half of his dog-food bill and half of Joe Miranda's gasoline bills when they went to matches in Joe's van.

Joe Miranda, that little Mex, had been a better partner than Deacon Gates. Cletus could drive over to Joe's place anytime he was free, take a look at the gray dog, have a beer or two, and jaw with Miranda. He missed Miranda. He was company, and that uppity Gates wasn't. Even if Gates hadn't been black, he wouldn't have been company.

Cletus's thoughts shifted to his own kinfolks. His brother Walt could go to the devil for all he cared. He wouldn't go out there to see him again, not after they'd taken Stella Jane away from him. Unless Walt and that smart-aleck wife of his got in his way, he wouldn't have anything more to do with them. And if they gave him any guff, he knew a way to take the starch out of them.

"I've got ol' Walt by the scruff, you bet!" Cletus told himself aloud. "I got Walt right where I want him. When I got his dog, I paid him back plenty for his uppityness. Wouldn't ol' Walt's eyes bug out, though, if he knew how much money that dog's made for me. He'll win tonight, too. Howie and

Miranda said he was the best they'd seen in years."

Cletus grinned at his beer can as he picked it up. "Yep, with the bets and all, I've made close to $9,000 on the mutt. That'll take me back to the folks in Arkansas, and it'll take me there in a new car with a new deer rifle and some fishin' gear. Their eyeballs'll pop. I'll tell 'em I struck it rich here in California, and they'll write that news back to Walt and Shirley. That'll gall the pair of 'em. I'll close up my shop and sell the tools here."

Cletus raised his can of beer as if he were making a toast. "Here's to the Staffordshire Terror. Here's hoping he wins for me tonight."

Yep, there'd be dogfighting in Arkansas and nearby states, too. When he got home, he'd look up his old pals and find out where the matches were held nowadays. With any luck at all he might be able to buy into a dog there. The country was full of dogs! All kinds of dogs. Let Deacon Gates have the gray terrier all to himself. The dog had been fun for a while, but he was tired of the mutt. He'd have more fun impressing the whole family back in Arkansas.

He might even bring them some presents, transistor radios for the grown-ups and toys for the young ones. He could move in with one of his kinfolks and not be lonesome anymore.

Cissie lay hidden for over an hour in the truck

until she heard the front door of the house shut and her dad coming down the front steps. A moment later the driver's door opened, then shut, and the truck's engine coughed into life.

They were off!

The journey down the old Benson Road was a bad one for Cissie, who lay on the hard metal truck bed without any padding under her. She bounced and slid around under the tarpaulin, bruising herself with almost every rut the pickup hit. She kept telling herself that it would be better when they got to the main road and from there onto the freeway that went to San Bernardino.

It was smoother and a little better on the main road, but she slid around until she caught hold of a metal ring her dad had bolted into the side of the truck bed so he could run a rope through it and tie loads in. When he brought Spook home to her, oh joy, she'd probably use this ring to hold a tether that she'd attach to his collar. Then she'd sit beside him all the way home, loving him and comforting him! She'd seen that he wore a spiky-looking collar, when she'd watched him fight the brown dog in the barn. Probably that Miranda man had put it around his neck.

Cissie was right. But little did she know the effort that had gone into getting the collar on the dog, the maneuverings with the electric prod, and how Miranda had finally managed by fastening a cloth over the terrier's clashing jaws till the chore was done. Afterward the collar had stayed on. It would never have been put on at all except that the rules at the dogfights required that the dogs be collared so their masters might have something to grab onto.

The pickup slowed down, then made a sudden sharp turn to the right that sent her sliding around. Cissie knew that her father was entering the freeway. There was a burst of speed, as he blended the pickup into the traffic, and then the whishing of wind from cars passing on either side of them. She could tell by the heavy gusts when big trucks went by. Some of them made the light pickup shudder and sent it drifting from its lane until her father, a good driver, eased it back.

She had no idea how long they had been on the road when he turned off to the right and began to drive more slowly. He drove for quite a distance, it seemed to her, and then he stopped the truck. Where were they now?

Cissie pulled herself to her knees and, lifting the tarpaulin, looked over the side of the truck. Her dad was headed for a phone booth beside a service station. She saw him look in the phone book, then put a dime into the slot, and start to dial. She couldn't hear him say quietly, "I want to report dogfighting at the old roadhouse at the end of Green Spot Road. . . . No, this ain't a joke. I don't mean a fight between two dogs. These are professional

194

dog matches with men comin' to 'em and placing bets. . . . My name is Walter Rose, and I live in Mira Loma on Benson Road. I'm in the phone book."

Cissie saw him hang up and start back to the pickup, and she sank down under the tarpaulin. He got in, started the engine, and then she felt the jerk of the truck as they went down Green Spot Road. He drove for about five minutes; then he parked again.

Cissie got up again to look out from under the canvas. Cars were parked in front of the pickup and on each side of it. There was a large building ahead, a sort of big old house, not a barn. In the moonlight it was a black bulk, dark all over, except for one end. That was yellow with light. There was a sign along the front of the building painted in white letters. The sign said *Dine and Dance* on it.

So that was what a roadhouse was, not just a house built alongside a road. She'd wondered about that. It was a sort of eating place and dance place at the same time.

She watched her father get out of the pickup, and at the same moment she heard a shouting and a roaring from inside the roadhouse. Cissie cringed, remembering where she'd heard just such a sound before: the barn near Colton.

The fights had started.

For certain, her dad had left to search among the

parked cars for the greenish-silver van Mr. Cameron had told him about. Was Spook inside it, or was he inside fighting?

Oh, how she hoped Spook wasn't fighting at this moment! How she hoped he was still inside the van or in a net somewhere safe. Lying on the truck's bottom, Cissie muttered a prayer that her dog would be safe as another cheer and a roar went up. She could not wipe out of her memory the fighting she'd seen in the barn, and she shivered, though the night was a warm one.

All at once other sounds started to come to her ears, the sounds of car engines. There were a number of cars driving up in silence and parking. She could hear them all around her.

Cissie risked another quick peek over the side. They were black-and-white and cream-colored police cars with lights on their roofs just over the driver's seat. Yet there were no lights at all to be seen now, except for the moonlight.

Periodically roars came from inside the building. Otherwise, it was all very, very quiet, so quiet it was scary.

Then all at once everything erupted! At a very loud shouted signal through a police bullhorn, all of the lights on the police cars were turned on at the same time—the headlights, spotlights, and the flashing red lights on top. In an instant it was bright

196

as noon around the roadhouse, and policemen in black uniforms and sheriff's men in tan ones stood outside their automobiles.

"Come on out! Come on out!" yelled the policeman with the bullhorn. "You're all under arrest for fighting dogs in there."

What a shouting came from the roadhouse, and a moment later the sirens started up on the police cars. There were no lights shining onto the truck Cissie was hidden in, so she didn't bother to conceal herself again. Breathless with excitement, she watched from under the tarpaulin, which she wore like a hood over her head. Only her eyes were visible over the top of the pickup's side.

She saw the men come out of the roadhouse with their hands up in the air and watched policemen make them stand away from their cars alongside the building with their hands clasped over their heads. At once she spotted the tall, elegantly dressed black man she'd seen before at the barn in Colton. He wore a pale blue suit tonight. He was herded over to stand near the big fat man whom she'd also seen at the fight in the barn. These two stood next to someone who was a stranger to her, a sour-faced, very well-dressed man with a neat brown beard.

And now she spotted the one she'd wanted most of all to see—her Uncle Cletus. He wasn't sour looking, but excited and sweating and sort of scared.

Unlike the others, he didn't come out the front door but crawled over the sill of a dark side window that was not lit by the police lights. Unseen by the officers, he moved at a crouching shamble between cars. Cissie watched him openmouthed as he started through the parked cars to her right, heading for another pickup truck, only a car away from the Rose truck. Sure as could be, he was hoping for a hiding place inside its back!

Cissie was speechless; she wanted to cry out but was tongue-tied with shock, not able to put her fury into words. She watched Cletus put his hand on the tailgate of the truck, and then saw her dad come hurtling out from behind another car to fling himself onto Cletus and shove him away from it.

She heard a name hissed, "Cletus!" Then she saw her father bring up his fist and hit his brother in the face. Down went Cletus. He didn't stay down, though. He was up in an instant, his nose bleeding, but full of fight all the same. Before he hit Walt Rose in return, he said in a low rumbling tone, "What're you doin' here, Walt? You let me be. Let me be if you know what's good for you."

"I won't let you be, Cletus! I've got my reasons for being here. You ain't gettin' away from me now."

Cissie heard her uncle snarl, "You got my Stella Jane away from me. I got plenty to settle with you,

Walt." His blow caught Walt Rose in the solar plexus, and he bent over for a moment that terrified the watching Cissie.

She heard her father say, grunting out the words as he straightened up, "Cletus, you stole my kid's pet dog, and maybe you'll be the cause of killing it if you don't get stopped. There wasn't any call for you to do that to my little girl. And you've caused me plenty of other bad trouble too. You know what I mean."

This time his left-handed jab hit the lower part of his brother's face. The blow was hard, and it made Cletus stagger back. He had had his fill of fist fighting with Walt, who was some years younger. Cletus raised a thick leg for a hard kick to his brother's stomach to stop him for good. But Walt Rose saw it coming and dodged. He caught the leg, twisted it, and Cletus fell abruptly onto the dusty, hard ground. As he lay there he grabbed his nose with one hand. Then Cissie heard her dad, standing over him, fists clenched and ready, speaking to him. The words were soft, meant only for his brother's ears. "You're a disgrace to our whole family, Cletus. Nobody anywhere ought to have to put up with you. Thank God Stella Jane got shed of you."

A moment later Cissie sank down again because she saw policemen rushing over to the pickup.

An officer demanded angrily, "What's going on

here? What're you two doing? Why is this man on the ground bleeding?"

Walt Rose explained, puffing, "Fighting. I punched his face. This is my brother, Cletus, Cletus Rose. I'm Walt Rose. I came here about a dog I think is inside the silver-green van over by the roadhouse. You just look inside it. I bet you'll find a dog in a cage. It ought to be a gray pit bulldog. My brother was trying to get away from you by hiding in this here red pickup, so I stopped him for you."

Cissie caught the suspicion in the policeman's voice, as he said, "You trying to say the two of you weren't inside at the fights then?"

Walt Rose explained quietly, "No, I wasn't in there, but my brother was. I saw him come out the side window, so I came through the cars to meet him."

Another officer interrupted. "So you say! You could have come out a back door or a window over by the creek behind the roadhouse."

Cissie heard the deeper voice of the third officer. "You guys could have been fighting out here because of some bet you made inside. Maybe your brother was running out on you, Rose."

The first policeman spoke again. "And there's another thing we'd like to know. If as you say, Walter Rose, you weren't inside at any time, how come you're outside the place where the dogs were fighting? Weren't you fixing to go inside when we showed up? What made you come here if it wasn't to see the dogfights?"

"No," said Cissie's father angrily. "I wasn't inside! I heard from somebody that there'd be dog-fighting and that I could find a dog that belongs to my family here. I came here about the dog. You can check me out with the police operator who answered the phone call I made to you to report the dogfights. I gave her my name and my Mira Loma address. Would I do that if I planned to go inside the road-house, knowing you would be coming? I came here to get our dog if I could. You can check my identi-fication if you want to."

There was a little silence until an officer asked, "Okay, I've seen your driver's license and your brother's too. Now tell us, Walt Rose, who told you about the fights tonight?"

"A Mr. Perry Cameron, my daughter's school-teacher. He overheard some men talking about the fights in a café last night."

One of the officers said, "That's a queer source, a schoolteacher. You know, it appears to me that a number of stories are pretty odd here. I think we ought to take the two of you men in with us tonight along with the others we caught inside the road-house."

While she listened, Cissie had been biting at her

thumb. Hearing what the officers just said made her gasp in horror. Wow, was her dad in big trouble now, and all because he was trying to help her! It sure wasn't fair. Not one bit fair!

Suddenly she clawed the tarpaulin off her, scrambled to her feet, and stood up in the truck bed. She cried out, "But he wasn't inside, though my Uncle Cletus was. We only came here, Dad and I, to get my dog back. You keep an eye on Uncle Cletus; he always sneaks away. Grab hold of him now."

"Good Lord!" exclaimed a policeman. Then he laughed, looking at Cissie illumined by the light of their flashlights.

Walt Rose thundered at her, "What're you doing here, girl? You musta snuck down from your room, didn't you? How'd you know where I was going tonight? You hid yourself in the pickup, and you came here without my knowing it. You're sure going to catch it good when I get you back home, Cissie Rose."

The officer with the deep voice laughed, too. "Yep," he said. "He's probably tellin' the truth. He didn't go inside. He wouldn't fetch his girl along to a dog meet and leave her out here all alone. She sneaked up there into the back of his truck." He turned briskly to Cletus Rose. "Okay, get up, you!" Then he spoke to Cissie's dad. "We'll take this brother of yours over to the other prisoners. Where's this van you were talking about just now? We'll want to check out your story about a dog."

"Just a minute," interrupted Cletus Rose in a growling rumble of anger, as he took his hand from his still trickling nose. "You're takin' my brother's word and his kid's word for everything! There's something you don't know about him that I do. Sure, he's my brother, Walt, Walt Rose, the family jailbird. He keeps his prison record awful quiet down here, keeping his nose clean as can be even if he just mashed mine. But all the same he spent some time in the penitentiary up in Washington State. That's his kid with him, all right. She's a sneak, for sure. She come here without his knowing it. Don't that prove what she's like? She thinks she's plenty smart, but I bet she don't know her pop's an ex-con." Cletus grinned in triumph as he felt in his back pocket for a bandana handkerchief.

"All right, you've told us your news," said one of the policemen. He turned to Walt as Cletus, who held the bandana to his nose, was led away by the two other officers to join the arrested men. "What's the story here?"

Cissie was frozen to the spot in the truck, staring down at her father's grim, set face, more deeply lined now than she'd ever seen it. Yes, it was true. She felt suddenly sick.

"Yes, I served out my sentence with time off for

good behavior. You can check me out. I never got in any more trouble anywhere," her father said slowly.

"We will. You can be sure of that. Okay, what about this van and dog? Who'd have the keys?"

"A black man. That's what her teacher said. That's all I know."

"There's only one black man over there. Let's go and ask him. Then we'll open up that van."

"Dad! Dad!" cried Cissie. "It's my dog! I have to go too!"

Walt Rose asked the policeman, "Can she go? It *is* her dog we came here for."

"Okay, as long as she doesn't get in the way."

So Cissie slid down over the fender onto the ground and ran after her father. The two Roses and the one officer started off together but halted in front of the group of prisoners. There the policeman demanded from Deacon Gates, "Have you got the keys to a green van?"

"Yeah." Sullenly Gates reached into his pants pocket and, scowling as he saw the end of his big plans for the future, gave his keys to the policeman. The only thing that made him feel any better was that Bell wouldn't be getting the dog he wanted, and Cletus wouldn't be getting the money he wanted. They would all be losers as much as he would.

204

"Come on," the policeman ordered Walt and Cissie Rose.

Three officers and Cissie and her father went through the parked cars to the Deacon's van, which was parked very near to the roadhouse's front door. As they walked, Walt Rose put his arm around Cissie's waist and pulled her close to him as she looked away from his unhappy face. At last she knew what her uncle had on her dad, why her mom hadn't wanted him dragged into Spook's disappearance. When had dad been in prison? Cletus had said it was when they were up in Washington State. Yes, of course. That time Mom had said he was in the Army. That's when he'd been away from home so long. He had been in jail then.

"Come along, Cissie," were his only words to her.

They were soon at the van, and the policemen were unlocking the rear doors.

A wild barking commenced immediately. At that most-welcome-in-the-world sound, Cissie forgot about her uncle's cruel words. She shrieked, *"Spook? Spook?"* Was her dog in there, or was it some other dog?

"Stand back, all of you," ordered one of the officers, as he opened the double doors. Another policeman stood by with his pistol drawn, though fortunately Cissie, interested only in the dog inside, didn't see him.

Her father did and tightened his hold on her to keep her from running forward. If the dog inside was vicious and there were no bars to keep him from attacking, Walt Rose knew the animal would be shot at once.

It would have to be, to protect the people.

"Spook! Spook!" cried Cissie, as the doors swung open.

Yes, it was a gray dog in the cage, a terrier. Yes, it was *her* dog plunging at the stout iron bars that lay between the two of them!

Once he saw the bars, the policeman put his pistol back into its holster. He could tell at a glance that they were strong enough to keep the dog inside the van.

All at once the plunging and barking ceased. There was a silence while the terrier sniffed, scenting the air. Next he cocked his head, and finally he came up to claw at the bars as if he wanted a door opened for him. A little whine of annoyance came from him, followed by the familiar sharp-toned, "Let me out now," yelp the entire Rose family knew so well. It was a sound Spook had used from puppyhood.

"Okay, Cissie. Go on." Walt Rose gently released his daughter.

Cissie went up to the cage and stood in front of it for a long moment, staring into her dog's eyes. Then, as he tried in vain to poke his head through

206

the narrow-set bars, she reached in to fondle his ears. He whined again. Her eyes brimmed with tears as she saw the scars along his side and legs, healed wounds from his fights.

"Oh, Spook! Poor Spook," was all she could say over and over in a soft whispering.

Her father standing behind her asked the policeman, "You can see that the dog belongs to her, can't you? Can she take him home with her now? There's rope to tie him to his collar in my truck. He ain't dangerous when he's with us, with her."

"Yeah, it does appear to be her dog, all right, but she can't take him. The laws says no. Not right away. Monday, maybe. There are other dogs here in vans and inside the roadhouse, remember? They're all going to have to be impounded and go to the Humane Society for a while. She'll have to prove this dog belongs to her and that you folks are of good moral character and that you won't be fighting this dog again." The officer who was speaking gave Walt Rose a suspicious glance out of the corner of his eye.

Cissie's father understood why. The police were wondering about the relationship between him and Cletus, one of whom had been inside the roadhouse and the other who claimed to have been outside, but who also said his family owned this fighting dog. And they were wondering about that jail sentence, too.

Walt Rose said, "Look, my girl raised this dog from a pup. She's crazy about him. Look at her now. The dog was stolen, and now she's found him. We wouldn't fight him again. We ain't about to set up fights for him. If I wanted to get him back to fight him, would I call you to come and raid this place? I gave my real name and address over the phone to the operator at the police station. This dog is our watchdog. All we want is to have him home with us again. We'd like to take him home right now, but if we can't, we can't."

"Okay, Rose." One of the officers was friendlier sounding. "What you say makes sense to me. She can take up matters with the folks at the Humane Society. Until then, though, this dog has to stay there. We'll try to find out about your dog being stolen later on, but don't expect anybody to confess to that."

Walt Rose came up to Cissie, who was whispering to Spook. The dog was listening attentively to her sweet soothing words. Her father rested his hand on her shoulder. "Cissie, I know you'll be getting your dog back real soon, but first he has to go to the pound for a little while. It's the law."

Cissie sighed. "All right, Dad. I guess I can wait another day or two as long as I know Spook won't be fighting." She put her hand through the bars to stroke the terrier's head and shoulders, and he licked it with his rough tongue.

The Roadhouse

Then she felt about in the pockets of her wind-breaker for something to give him as a token. Out came a grubby pink handkerchief that had been in there for weeks, because she kept forgetting to put it in the laundry hamper. "Here," she said, pushing it through the bars, "smell this when you get lone-some, Spook. It ought to smell just like me. I snif-fled in it plenty while you were gone. Don't you worry, Spook. I'll get you real, real soon. I'll call somebody up about you and get you right away."

As Cissie turned away from the cage to her father, Spook suddenly let out a long, lonesome howl that made one of the policemen grin. He motioned to another to watch the fierce fighting terrier as Spook padded over to the handkerchief and carefully picked it up in his teeth.

The second policeman chuckled as Spook went to a corner of his cage to lie down, looking quite fool-ish, with the pink handkerchief in his jaws. Then the officer said, "Let's shut up the van again and wait for somebody to come to drive it to the dog pound."

Cissie didn't look back at her dog, nor did she look at her uncle, Gates, Mr. Bell, and Fat Howie in the group of arrested men. She walked calmly past them, ignoring them; then suddenly she ran for the family pickup. Jerking open the door, she got into the seat and sat down, waiting for her father to join her.

The Staffordshire Terror

The Roses rode home in silence until they turned onto the road where Walt Rose had struck the female terrier months before. As they passed the spot, he cleared his throat and said, "Cissie, I was in prison, but I behaved myself and I got time off for good behavior. I want to tell you all about it now. After a quick trial before a tough judge, I went to prison up in Washington State because the police there found auto parts that had been stolen from a Seattle garage in the radiator shop Cletus and I had. The police came there earlier to look for a stolen car. Cletus had fired the mechanic who was supposed to have it, but the police must have seen something that made them suspicious. Cletus had left town by the time they came back to the shop, but not me. I didn't know then that those auto parts had been stolen, but I think Cletus knew when he got 'em so dirt cheap. The judge refused to believe me when I said I didn't ever know they were stolen and didn't know where Cletus had got them."

All at once Cissie slid over the seat and snuggled against her father. "Don't feel bad about it anymore, Dad. Uncle Cletus'll be the jailbird now, and I think maybe you busted his nose because it bled so much. It doesn't matter anymore to us where you were up in Washington, Dad."

"Oh, yes, it does matter, honey. Mr. Benson maybe won't be wanting an ex-convict working for him on his place. That's what your mother thinks, and so do I. We've been worried that word about me might get out ever since Cletus showed up here."

"That's why you didn't like seeing him come here, huh?"

"Yes. We didn't ever want him to look us up."

"Why is he so mean to you?" Cissie wanted to know.

Walt Rose sighed deeply as he swung the truck onto the old Benson Road. "He was the oldest of the four of us brothers. He had to go to work when he had only a year of high school to help support all of us when our dad passed away. My brothers and I were lucky enough to get a couple of years of high school. That galled Cletus. When I married a woman who'd gone all the way through high school, that galled him even more. He thought she acted very superior to him, because she talked different and read books. I feel sorry about the life your mom's had with me, particularly up in Washington. I tried to shelter her here from more trouble as much as I could, Cissie, but now she has to hear the whole story. I have to tell her what Cletus said about me in front of the police and about what happened to Spook's mother. It's time for the whole thing to come out now."

"I guess so, Dad." Cissie sighed also.

"Cissie, it appears to me that you've got some tall talking to do, explaining about some things I don't know about. How did you know where I was really going tonight when I left the house?"

"I heard you and Mr. Cameron talking because I was up on the roof. Sure, Dad, I'll explain things like who the real owner of Spook and his mother is. I found out, you know! I even talked with him in Riverside, and I have his phone number and a promise from him." Cissie managed a little laugh. "Dad, you'd better tell Mom why you haven't got the chain saw with you when you said you were going out for it tonight."

When Cissie got up the next morning, she arose with the feeling that she'd been robbed. The joy of getting Spook back had been stolen from her by what her uncle had said and by the memory of her mother's tear-streaked face the night before when she heard her husband's story and then Cissie's longer one.

More unhappiness appeared later that morning when Lita, who'd been told before breakfast that Spook had been found, called Mark with the good news. Mark's father was a lawyer and told Mark that the men who had been arrested for dogfighting would only be jailed for about six weeks. They'd be let free a lot sooner if they could put up bail for their release.

Lita repeated that phone conversation with a very sour face to Cissie, Darrell, and Mrs. Rose. Cissie's father wasn't there to hear it. According to her mother, he'd got up at dawn and gone out to the barn without breakfast. Cissie guessed how he must feel. He didn't want to see anybody because he was upset and worried about his job. She could see, too, why he wasn't hungry. Neither was she.

Cissie exploded when she heard Lita's angry, disappointed news. "Six weeks! That's all those men will get? Six weeks for hurting dogs! I'd give 'em six years! I'd like to see old Uncle Cletus stay in jail twice that long."

Mrs. Rose was shaking her head as she cooked a second pancake for Darrell. "Cletus must have made money fighting Spook," she said. "He won't be in jail any six weeks. He'll get out as soon as possible. It wouldn't surprise me if he bailed himself out by noon tomorrow."

"Oh, no, Mom!" Cissie's face crumpled with misery.

"That's bad," came from Lita.

"You're right. It is bad. But it's true. He could be out by then."

Darrell muttered angrily as he attacked the pancake his mother put onto his plate from the skillet. "Oh, who cares about him anyhow? He won't have Spook to fight for him again, and he won't be coming out here anymore to pester us. I wish we could nail old Uncle Cletus for a big, old dog stealer, too."

Cissie's eyes met her mother's sadly over Darrell's bent head. Darrell had been asleep when she and her father had come home the night before. Lita had been out on a date with Mark. Darrell and Lita knew part of the story, but not what Uncle Cletus had said about his brother to the police. Cissie hoped in her heart that Darrell would never learn about his dad being in jail. She wouldn't ever tell him, but she was going to tell Lita later on. Her dad had told her to when she'd asked him last night if she should.

Cissie went to sit with Lita in the porch swing after the two of them had done the breakfast dishes. Sitting, swinging back and forth, Cissie told her cousin about her dad having been in prison.

Lita's response gladdened her a bit. "I just know your dad didn't do that, Cissie. I know that he's innocent. Yes, I thought he was in the Army then, too. Boy, is your mom ever a brave lady! She sure kept it quiet, and, remember, I lived in the same house with her all along. I never even guessed that he wasn't overseas. She got letters from your dad where she worked as a waitress, but she never showed 'em or read from them. She's sure a good actress. She never even went to visit him. I guess she was afraid we'd find out if she did go. She said she kept the letters in her locker where she worked." Lita sighed, then changed the subject. "If I know that awful old Cletus, and I sure do, he's going to run fast as he can to tell Mr. Benson about your dad being in prison the minute he gets out of jail himself. I sure wish we could help your dad."

"So do I, Lita." Cissie lay back in the swing with her eyes closed. A lot of things were very clear to her now about her dad's feelings toward his brother Cletus. It wasn't just the overdue bills and the bad checks Cletus wrote and his way of treating Stella Jane. It was stolen goods and jails and the threat hanging over her dad's head all the time Cletus had been there. It wasn't one bit fair. Not fair at all!

Cissie said finally, "Lita, Mr. Cameron says Mr. Benson's a real nice man. He was sure nice to me yesterday."

"Yes, he is. And your dad likes him, too. That's why it would be so tough to leave this place, even if we go to live in Riverside."

Cissie went on, "You didn't hear him talking yesterday, but Mr. Benson doesn't only want Dad to take care of this place, he wants him to plant potatoes and farm for him." She got up to lean against the porch post. "I think Mr. Benson likes us a whole lot."

Cissie left the front porch slowly, starting up to her room. She didn't go up the stairs, though. She loitered in the hallway not far from the telephone. Then suddenly she went up to it and stared at the short list of frequently called numbers tacked up beside it. She ran her finger down them, stopping at the third one.

Cissie took the receiver off the wall phone and, with her lips moving and her eyes closed tight, held it for a moment against her chest. Then slowly she began to dial, first a 6, then an 8, then a 4.

All at once she put the receiver back into its cradle. "It isn't fair. It just isn't fair!" she said under her breath.

She took the receiver down again. This time her whole arm and hand were trembling as she began to dial once more. The 6, the 8, the 4, then 5, and afterward the final three numbers.

When she heard the phone ringing, she put her free hand up to her mouth to chew on the knuckles. "Be there. Oh, be home," she whispered. "Please, be there!"

"Hello," came the voice from the other end of the line.

"Hello, Mr. Benson, it's me, Cissie Rose."

"Who is it? I can barely hear you. Speak up, please."

Cissie raised her voice. "It's me, Cissie Rose. I hate to bother you, but I have something awful important to tell you."

"All right, go ahead, Cissie."

"It'll take ten minutes maybe. Have you got that long for me?"

216

"Yes, I have ten minutes. I might even have more than that on a Sunday morning."

"It's not about the chain saw or the potatoes."

"There are other things in the world besides chain saws and potatoes. I doubt if you'd call me up about them in any event. Now you've stirred up my curiosity. What's on your mind?"

Nobody heard Cissie's soft conversation except the man on the other end of the line, though she talked for more than fifteen minutes. At first her voice was strained and choked, and the hand that held the receiver was stiff with tension, but as the talking went on she grew more and more relaxed. At the end she was leaning against the wall the way Lita often did when she talked to Mark.

The final words Cissie heard brought a broad smile to her face. "Well, well, you sure are a fine spunky girl in my estimation! Your dad's a lucky man to have such a daughter. I just wish I had. Don't you worry. I understand. Your father's the best caretaker I ever had out there. I like him, and I like all of you. No, I'm not going to fire your father because his no-good brother made trouble for him and got him into prison. If that Cletus gets in touch with me about this, you can be sure that I'll tell him where to get off. You folks stop worrying and go on taking good care of my property. That's all I ask. You tell your dad to plant lots of potatoes and come to town to get the chain saw before the pepper tree splits wide open and takes off half the roof with it. There's no need at all for me to mention prison to him or to anybody else."

After Cissie had said, "Oh, thank you, thank you!" and hung up the receiver, she raced down the hallway through the living room and over the front porch. Passing a startled Lita, Cissie flew across the yard between the barn and the house.

As she ran, she shouted, "Dad! Dad! Mr. Benson says everything's all right. *He knows*! I told him just now over the phone. He wants you to go get the chain saw and to plant lots and lots of spuds."

Looking as startled as Lita, Walt Rose came out of the barn to catch Cissie as she launched herself at him, laughing.

"What is it, Cissie?"

"It's okay, Dad. Everything is all right. Mr. Benson says he wants you to stay on here and work for him. I just called him on the phone, and I told him what Uncle Cletus had said and that Cletus might be calling him to tell him about you. Everything's okay. Mr. Benson's going to tell Uncle Cletus to get off if he calls him saying you were in jail."

"Cissie! Well, well!" The sudden smile on her dad's face matched Cissie's own, and all at once they looked alike.

He said, "First, you show up like the U.S. Cavalry in the pickup last night just in time to rescue me,

218

and now you go and call Mr. Benson all on your own. I planned to see him tomorrow and tell him myself, but you beat me to it!"

"Oh, Dad, we *all* beat Uncle Cletus! You and Mom and Lita and me, and Spook, too, in a way, because he'll soon be free now. We're rid of Cletus for good! He hasn't got a hold on you anymore. I bet he leaves the town, but if he ever comes out here, there's only three words he ever ought to hear from any one of us Roses or from Lita."

"What would they be, honey?" asked Walt Rose, laughing.

Cissie flung back her head, then held him tight around his waist as she cried, "They sure aren't 'I love you.' They're 'Sic him, Spook!' "

Anna
+
Angel.

Author's Note

When they hear the word *dogfight,* most people smile as if to say such a thing is of very little importance. That humorous expression about a despised piece of clothing, "I wouldn't wear that to a dogfight," typifies the common opinion.

Dogfighting is illegal, but it is a well-regulated business across the United States, and it is a growing business. Law-enforcement officials estimate that there are nearly 5,000 men who meet at secret locations all over the nation to fight their animals and bet at dogfights. There are even underground magazines devoted to this "sport." Some of them list the names of the dogs featured on the program. Dogs who have won as many as ten to twelve fights are known nationwide.

The purebred Staffordshire terriers, also known

220

in the United States as pit bulldogs and bullterriers, were bred for centuries in England for their fighting qualities, and they are considered to have the most powerful jaws of any breed. Bullterriers are fancied as fighting dogs in this country but like all purebred dogs they are valuable and expensive. Mongrels are also used and other purebreds such as St. Bernards, huskies, Malamutes, German shepherds and Dobermans.

Male dogs are matched against male dogs and females against females. Some of the fighting dogs have been trained by tantalizing them with cats in mesh bags. Fighting dogs are remarkably thin, not because they are underfed, but because their owners want to keep them at a certain fighting weight. Because they are often vicious, they aren't exercised in public on leashes like ordinary dogs but on treadmills. Most are not fed canned dog food but raw meat, which is thought not only to keep their weight down but also to increase their fighting spirit.

The secret pits are portable enclosures, consisting of a carpet with a tarpaulin over it and a plyboard wall fifteen feet square and three feet high. Sometimes the dog's owner goes into the pit with him when he fights.

As anyone who has ever seen a neighborhood dogfight can testify, it is a noisy affair. Not so the matches held between fighting dogs. People who have seen them remark on the eerie silence. The chief sound to be heard is that of the scratching of the dog's claws on the tarpaulin. Experienced animals are often famous for a particular brand of fighting. They are known to "work the stifle" (get another dog by the throat) or "work the legs" or "work the ears." Ear dogs are considered the best of the lot and accordingly are worth a great deal of money.

In this book, I have deliberately toned down the two fights my Staffordshire terrier takes part in, and I have made them mercifully brief. In actuality a pair of dogs can fight from half an hour to two and a half hours, constantly chewing, slashing, and biting. Badly mauled dogs do not generally die during the fight. They die afterward of internal injuries and dehydration from exertion and loss of blood.

The men who attend these fights and bring their dogs to them are by custom known only by their first names and the city or state they hail from. This precaution is taken, of course, because staged dogfights are illegal.

What of the legal penalties for men caught involved in fighting dogs or attending dogfights? For the most part, law officials claim they are nowhere heavy enough. Sometimes, as in the case of the also illegal cockfighting, there are jail sentences, but men can often post bail and be released. If they are convicted in court, they receive fines that seldom run higher than $500, an amount comparable to a common bet on one dogfight.

There is another feature to dogfighting that is seldom realized by people who agree that it is a brutal business and should carry heavy criminal penalties. They have not considered what happens to the dogs after the police raid the matches and take the spectators and dog owners off to jail. The confiscated dogs are transferred to the local Humane Society and boarded, for a time. They are almost always destroyed. Because of their savage natures, such dogs are not taken to homes as pets or even as watchdogs.

Patricia Beatty
January 1979

About the Author

Now a resident of Southern California, Patricia Beatty was born in Portland, Oregon. She was graduated from Reed College there, and then taught high-school English and history for four years. Later she held various positions as science and technical librarian and also as a children's librarian. Quite recently she has taught Writing Fiction for Children in the Extension Department of the University of California, Los Angeles. She has had a number of historical novels published by Morrow, several of them dealing with the American West in the 1860 and 1895 period.

With her late husband, Dr. John Beatty, Mrs. Beatty also coauthored a number of books. One of them, *The Royal Dirk,* was chosen as an Award Book by the Southern California Council on Children's and Young People's Literature. Subsequently Mrs. Beatty received another award from the Council for her Distinguished Body of Work.

Mrs. Beatty is now married to a professor of economics at the University of California, Riverside, and she has a married daughter, Alexandra Beatty Stewart.